JAMESY HARPER'S

BIG BREAK

Julianne Harvey

Ruby
Finch
BOOKS
intuitive courage

This is a work of fiction. Names, characters, places, events, and incidents are either products of the author's imagination or are used fictitiously. Any resemblance to actual events, or persons, living or dead, is purely coincidental.

Cover design by Dani Compton
Book design by First Choice Books
Author Photo by William Harvey

Published by Ruby Finch Books, Vancouver, BC, Canada

www.rubyfinchbooks.com

ISBNs 978-0-9877978-2-7 (paperback) and
978-0-9877978-3-4 (ebook)

10 - 9 - 8 - 7 - 6 - 5 - 4 - 3 - 2

Printed and bound by First Choice Books & Victoria,Bindery
Victoria, BC, Canada

www.firstchoicebooks.ca

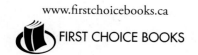 FIRST CHOICE BOOKS

For Ava, the best daughter and actor in the world

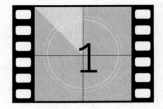

INT. CASTING OFFICE — DAY

JAMESON HARPER (16) stands in front of a camera, delivering lines in character as GEMMA BEEKDAL, with an earnest expression.

                    BEEKDAL
    This is the last time I'm going to say
    this, Franny.
                    (beat)
    You are not going to make it out of this
    room unless you give me the combination
    to the safe.

                    FRANNY
                    (crying)
    I… I …I don't know it. I'm not lying, I
    swear!

                    BEEKDAL
    Dammit, Franny, I'm waiting.

The CASTING DIRECTOR (35) stands, motioning at the CAMERAPERSON (22) to cut with her hand waving at her throat.

                    CASTING DIRECTOR
                       (big smile)
          Fabulous job, Jamesy. Nice work. Poor
          Franny.

Everyone in the room laughs. Jamesy gathers her coat from a chair and exits.

→ ←

As I walk to the bus, rain dripping down my face like Franny's fake tears, I attempt to balance out my scalp-tingling joy at how well that audition went with my usual rage thoughts on a loop. My God, this pursuing-your-dreams lark would be easier if my parents actually drove me around and cheered me on like they are supposed to. By the time I get to my bus stop, I'm wet and shivering. I pry my Compass Card out of my phone case and flash it at the sensor on the bus, noticing that my best friend Lawrence has texted as I thread my way through the eclectic group of bus people. As soon as I plunge down onto the hard, blue plastic bench, I click to see what's up.

> Hey sexy drama sucks donkey balls without you
> why u gotta leave me alone in this hell while
> you become some Julia Roberts type A-list shit

So, not critically important, then. I'm thrilled to see he's utilized only one "u," as we came to an agreement after Christmas that I'll indulge his retro '80s fetish if he'll text me in proper English to avoid sounding like a moronic teenager in real life as well as online. His punctuation is hopeless so I've given up on that. I'm cooking up a snarky response when my phone buzzes with my mom's frowning face on the smudgy screen. My heart rate ticks upwards as I punch decline and look out the window. Val has already called twice—once while I was waiting for the audition and then again while I was performing. Somewhere in my subconscious I can feel her trying to tank my chances. My Grandpa Butch is always telling me that Val does these irritating things because she loves me, but my standard response is, "You know how else she could reveal her love? BY DRIVING ME TO AUDITIONS."

I take a deep breath, remembering how proficient and strong I felt walking out of that casting office earlier. Sure, it was my thirty-seventh audition since I signed with my agent, Sam, nearly a year ago, but I know I'm inching closer to that "yes" with every goddamn "no" I hear. With a dream as big as this one, it's not supposed to be easy, or everyone would be doing it. The reason it's hard is because the not quitting is where the winning is. Or at least that's what I tell myself when everything feels overwhelming and hopeless.

I shift my heavy backpack on my lap and think about pulling out a novel to read. I should be doing my science homework, but it can wait. I'm making my way through the Stephen King canon now that I've finished all of Jodi Picoult's weepers. Val still gets middle school and tame YA books out of the library for me. She prefers to believe I'll stay innocent forever. I leave her choices on my nightstand with a decoy Hufflepuff bookmark while secretly reading whatever the hell I want to read.

I decide to watch the wet Vancouver streets from the bus window instead. It's April, with cherry blossoms Pepto-Bismol pink on the budding trees, and I remind myself that today could be the day I get the "yes" I've been longing for. Then Val will stop harassing me and take notice of her daughter's talent. My dad, Edward, might leave work early one day to drive me so I don't have to spend forever on a bus. And supercilious Brooklyn, who used to be my elementary BFF but now flits around high school like a queen bee adored by her subjects, will actually be jealous of me.

> Heading to work. Phone sketchy on the bus. Home by 9:30

(Take that, Val. If my whereabouts are so important to you, try driving me to my auditions and showing some support for my dreams, even if you think acting is a one-way ticket to being homeless on skid row.)

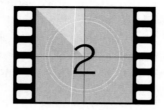

My clothes have mostly dried from the rain as I run down the steps of the bus in front of Lantern Cinemas, where I'll change into my burgundy-and-purple work golf shirt with a glowing lantern drawing the eye directly to my left boob. I've had this job for the last five months, and my glorious minimum wage paycheque, combined with cash from babysitting, have paid for the headshots, acting classes, and bus passes that my parents won't cover.

I struggle with the heavy glass door and walk inside, giving my eyes a minute to adjust to the dim interior. The smell of stale, burnt popcorn and musty carpets greets me like an old friend. One day, my movies will be playing here. Jameson Harper, former Lantern employee, will fly in from LA to do a special Q&A on opening night. She won't be too important to remember her roots and thank those who supported her in the early days of her storied career. I spend most of my shifts imagining some version of these events, and it certainly helps speed up the time.

After I dump my turquoise backpack in the employee lounge and don my polyester Lantern shirt, I come back to the lobby to find Grace refilling the paper in the debit machine. She's in her mid-fifties, I'd guess, but Grace enjoys dressing as though she's a college freshman. I love this about her. She gives zero fucks about society's expectations of how middle-aged women should look or dress. Her hair is dyed ash blonde, and she smokes like a chimney to keep her weight down (how her bone-dry hair doesn't ignite every time she lights up is beyond the physics of science). Grace has owned the Lantern for the last decade and prides herself on "keeping it vintage" (AKA "not spending a dime on the place"). She's an entertaining person and a chill boss.

"Hey Jamesy! How goes it? Did you come from school or an audition?"

I move behind the counter to restock paper cups, straws, and napkins before the Tuesday discount-matinee crowd arrives. "I had an audition for a new TV show. A small part, and the dialogue was gonzo, but it was fun, and I have a solid feeling about this one."

Grace snaps the cover down on the debit machine. "It's just a matter of time, Jamesy. We all know that." She pats my hand, like my Granny Dot used to, then walks around the counter toward her office in the back.

I bloom under her praise, like a plant being watered. In addition to Grace, my drama teacher Mrs. Wu and my stellar Grandpa Butch offer me enough bite-sized tidbits of approval to continue with acting. In another life I could've been Grace's child instead of Val's—then it would all seem easier.

Footsteps echo around the old lobby as Cole comes down from the projection room. Instant butterflies crowd the base of my throat. He trained me when I first started, and the last month or so Grace has been scheduling us for the same shifts. Perhaps she can see the chemistry that seems to be growing between us. It feels like a living thing—a simmering heat that neither of us knows quite what to do with.

He rounds the corner into the lobby and grins when he sees me. "Buddy," he says, to which I respond on cue, "Buddy." Cole comes to stand beside me, his tanned forearm brushing against mine. I look down at his scuffed brown boots, too breathless to look into those greenish eyes below that flippy brown hair. He'll turn eighteen in August, so some might think he's too old for me at sixteen (ahem...Val), but when his comforting presence stands so very close, nothing matters except that I want more of him.

The door opens, ushering in the first customers, and we have no more time to talk/flirt. I handle tickets while Cole makes popcorn. Our rhythm is smooth and practiced behind this counter. From down the line of patrons I can hear Brooklyn's high-pitched voice, clear and piercing. "I'm shooting that movie-of-the-week on Friday and next week my agent has me running to auditions and callbacks almost every day. I don't know how I'm ever going to keep up with homework. You guys have to help me… it's so stressful!"

(Oh my stars—I do declare. Why does Brooklyn speak like a southern belle in a *Gone with the Wind*-type movie?!) I know this because Grace adores anything set in the old days and hosts every-other-Saturday matinee showings of Golden Age cinema. There might be five seniors who attend, on a good day, but I've seen my share of Clark Gable, Ava Gardner, and Jimmy Stewart since I got this job. Brooklyn's ridiculous airs are fake on every level, but the suck-up popular girls she surrounds herself with eat it up with a designer spoon. I guess they've banked on her making it big so they can be her semi-famous entourage. Too bad they've bet on the wrong actor.

Now they are in front of me holding out cash, cheery smiles all around. "Missed you in drama today, Jamesy," Brooklyn squeaks. "How did the audition go? I had mine for that part last week."

"It was fantastic. May the best actor land it."

The entourage giggles as if my comment is hysterical. What's it like going through life so easily entertained, I wonder? Brooklyn passes me a crumpled twenty-dollar bill. My hand appears doughy and giant next to her dainty brown one. In grade eight I suddenly shot up to five feet seven, and she stayed tiny at five feet. Brooklyn's got that irritating stick-thin body type that Hollywood is so enamoured with. Her face hasn't been ravaged by teenaged zits like mine has lately. Where's the fairness in this? How do I have Val's gently rounded body and Edward's youthful bad skin when Brooklyn gets to win the genetic lottery AND have parents that think her burgeoning acting career is something to be celebrated instead of shunned?

When Cole brings over a popcorn and a small root beer, I take some pleasure in nudging my body up against his. Brooklyn smiles at Cole, dropping her head and looking up under her lashes at him like Scarlett Fucking O'Hara, but he doesn't seem to notice. We turn to the next customers in line and I'm determined not to let Brooklyn piss me off.

The movie starts, and when the last matinee stragglers have disappeared inside, I pull my phone out of my jeans and have a look. Lawrence messaged, wondering why I didn't answer him before about missing drama, Val called two more times (honestly, woman, dial down your panic levels, please) and there's a text below this noise from Sam, my agent. Sam is awesome. She's in her mid-twenties and just starting out as a junior agent, which makes her motivated and excitable. I like to think that we are friends. Everything slows down around me and inside me, nearly to a standstill, while I read.

> **Jamesy! Casting emailed from** *Code Breakers*. **You really impressed them. Callback Friday at 1:15. Congrats!!**

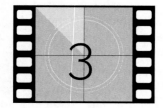

After work, around ten o'clock (as Lantern Cinemas doesn't do late shows on weeknights), I'm rummaging in our kitchen pantry for some snacks. Quiet stealth is the goal here, as I'm still buzzing from Sam's thrilling news, and the last thing I want is for Val or Edward to interrupt me and bring me thudding back to earth. My homework is spread out on the table but I'll take it up to my room if/when it's discovered that I'm home.

We live in a townhouse in White Rock, British Columbia. My younger brother, Tim, wants to have a huge house to impress people, but that doesn't appeal to me. Especially when Val makes us clean on the weekend. The smaller the place equals the sooner we are done. I prefer cozy spaces. Val shares Tim's opinion and has been at Edward for years that we should be upgrading from this "starter" townhouse into a "more upscale" neighbourhood.

I take three Oreos, a banana, and a glass of milk to the table. Both of my grey tabby cats (Crockett and Tubbs—my '80s-obsessed pal Lawrence suggested these names after he insisted we stream episodes of *Miami Vice*) are sprawled around my books and binders, trying ferociously to drink from my *Les Misérables* glass. I sit down carefully on my wooden chair, but damn if the laminate flooring doesn't betray me with a squeak.

Edward's voice floats up from the bonus room downstairs, where I can hear Jeff Probst calling out the play-by-play of a *Survivor* challenge. My parents never watch anything live because they think commercials are evil. They consider the PVR the greatest invention of all time. "James? Is that you?"

Probst is muted and in seconds both of my parents are in the kitchen. Suddenly I feel like I can't get enough air in my lungs.

Edward is tall and rangy, like my grade six brother is shaping up to be. He has thick salt-and-pepper hair, gradually more salty than peppery, but being married to Val can age an affable guy faster. He offers me a quick wink, as if to remind me that he's on my side throughout whatever is coming. Edward comes to grab one of my cookies, but I can predict his moves and sweep it off the table with one hand while protecting my milk from the bad cats with the other.

Val steps forward to wave her hand at Crockett and Tubbs. They watch her warily and jump down before she makes contact. She crosses her arms across her chest and stares me down. Her shoulder-length hair is a dirty blonde shade, similar to mine, but her eyes are a sharp blue instead of the unique hazel that came to me from some long-lost relative in our bloodline. "Jameson. We allow you to have a phone so you can be in contact with us, especially when you are gallivanting God knows where, and when you don't answer, it's reasonable for us to be worried about you. I would like to ask, yet again, for you to be considerate and answer your phone when I call."

"I was quite busy today with school, an audition for a role in a TV show, a six-hour shift at Lantern and now homework. I texted so you knew I was fine." (And since no cops showed up at the door, you could've safely guessed that even without the text.) I draw a deep breath and focus on Edward. "My agent told me that I've been booked for a callback on Friday for this part. This is as close as I've ever been to landing a paying role and I'm wildly excited."

Edward reaches out for a fist bump. "Good job, Skittles. You've worked hard for this. I hope you get it."

"Thanks, Dad." He beams for a second. I started referring to my parents by their first names when I turned thirteen, but I still honour him with "Dad" every so often when I'm feeling warm and fuzzy.

I'm afraid to turn to Val. However, this is momentous news so maybe there will be a crack in her armour. But no, her mask of displeasure is still firmly in place. "You know what I think about this, Jameson. Your academics are top priority, not some wild goose chase after fame and fortune. It's our job to see you succeed as an adult, and a practical career is the best way to make that happen."

Her words wash over me, as they have repeatedly over the last year, splashing into the broken places. I gather my homework with leaden arms and head to the bottom of the stairs.

"Don't worry. I'm not asking for anything from you. I can manage just fine on my own."

Edward sighs. I can imagine Val turning her frustration toward him and I don't want to hang around to see it. Ed's on his own. I start up the stairs to my bedroom, each step heavier than the last.

Wednesday, April 25th

Math class. How can any seventy-five-minute block feel so damn long? If any class is going to drag down my A average, it'll be this one. Mr. Sandringham speaks like he's under water, every word drawn out and unintelligible. (Come on, bell. Ring.)

Next up is drama, my favourite class. I can't wait to tell Mrs. Wu about my callback for *Code Breakers*. I won't do this in front of the whole class, jackass-style, the way Brooklyn announces her acting news. I'll find a quiet moment to tell her. Hopefully Mrs. Wu will run lines with me at lunch or after school to help me prepare. I really, really, really want to land this one.

Finally! The harsh buzzer sounds, springing me from this hell. I stuff my textbook and binder into my morbidly obese backpack and join the swell of high-schoolers teeming in the halls. Out of nowhere, Lawrence appears to hip check me with his usual flair. "Survive math?"

"Barely. How was woodshop?"

"Oh, you know. So manly. Every nail I pound proves something to my dad."

I laugh. Lawrence has an ongoing horror of societal norms. He tries to break them, but never in front of his evangelical Christian parents. I've known Lawrence since grade four when he moved to BC from small-town Saskatchewan, and every year he's a reinvented version of himself (or possibly shedding enough of the false variations to inch nearer to his real self). His dad is white, his mom is Black, and his skin is a perfect blend of both. Today he's wearing a forest-green mesh tank top over a ripped white tasselled T-shirt, jean shorts that Val would call "nasty Daisy Dukes" and black combat boots. I know he didn't leave the house looking like this, but I love the originality. Lawrence makes my wild ambitions seem reasonable and achievable.

"Should I announce your callback to the class so you don't have to?" Lawrence asks, as we walk into our drama room.

"No thanks. I'll leave that to Brooklyn." He raises his eyebrows at me.

Brooklyn approaches us from her spot in the corner. "Leave what to Brooklyn?" She smiles, but I can sense steel under it.

"Taking the lead in today's improv group," I lie with a practiced smoothness.

"That's generous of you, Jamesy." Brooklyn sips from her Broadway Playbill water bottle and straightens her lace skirt. "Hear anything back from *Code Breakers*?"

"Nothing yet," I say, before Lawrence can chime in. My pulse speeds up as I think about my first big callback. I don't want anything jinxing this. It's none of Brooklyn's business.

Students are still making their way in, so before the bell rings I squeeze Lawrence's bony elbow and corner Mrs. Wu by her desk. The drama room is my favourite place. It's papered in cheesy inspirational posters with cats and rabbits telling you not to quit and to be the best you possible. It smells of stale sweat, coffee, and baked goods in here. The atmosphere is one of hopeful possibility. Just breathing it in lifts my spirits.

"Mrs. Wu?" I whisper before she can move away. "My agent told me last night I've got a callback on Friday for a TV show part. I had to tell you."

"Oh Jameson, that's terrific. Simply amazing news. I'm so proud of you."

She moves close, her vanilla scent drifting over me. Joy rises from some buried inner treasure chest. "Can you run lines with me at lunch tomorrow?"

"Sure. Come here at twelve fifteen, and we'll get you ready to kill it."

She offers me a high-five. I look past Mrs. Wu to see Brooklyn watching us. I don't owe her any explanations. (It's not so easy, is it Brooklyn, when someone is getting their moment and it's not you? I had to deal with it when you started booking—now it's your turn.)

The bell is about to ring, and I dart out into the hall to hit the bathroom (that's my cover if an authority figure asks, but really I'm checking my phone to see if Sam's got me another audition). I slip my phone back into my pocket as the bell drills again, keeping order in the high school universe. I'm stopped by Ms. Kuntz, my science teacher, who is hurrying down the hall with a tall mug of coffee and an armful of papers. (She's always quick to say, "It's pronounced Koontz," but I'm sure you can guess the way students say it when she's not around.) "Did you get the readings and homework on the structure of atoms from a friend for yesterday? It's due tomorrow."

"Don't worry, Ms. K. I'll get it done. But I've got an acting callback for a TV show Friday afternoon so I'll miss science again. Can you email me what I need to do to catch up, and I'll work on it this weekend?"

Ms. Kuntz frowns, making her look like a caricature of an old-fashioned schoolmarm, with her white hair and her ramrod posture. "I don't want you to fall behind, Jameson. It's the end of the semester and we've got lots to do. Try not to miss too much school. I'll have to reach out to your parents if your grades start to fall because you can't keep up."

"Oh, please don't do that. I'll be okay. I've got eighty-six right now, so I'm holding at an A. It's good of you to be concerned, but I can handle it."

She carries on down the hall and I allow myself a small sigh. As long as Val doesn't hear from Ms. Kuntz I'll be alright. I hurry into drama to join my improv group and push everything else out of my mind for the next hour and fifteen minutes.

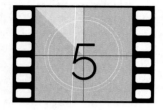

After school I'm on the 451 bus to the Sunny Acres Senior's Residence to visit Butch. (He got this nickname when Tim was little and complained about how boring his name was. Grampa asked, "What name would you like to be called instead?" and Tim said, "Butch." I don't remember this, but apparently the adults all fell about laughing, and we started referring to Grampa as Butch, instead.) I wish Butch lived with us, but we don't have extra space in our townhouse.

He says he loves it at Sunny Acres, but privately I wonder if he thinks we've abandoned him. The seniors have more programming there than I have in high school, so Butch certainly isn't bored. He goes on field trips to museums and art galleries, plays card bingo three times a week, gets into long, heated debates with residents and staff about crime novels and old western movies, plus he naps at two every single day. Last winter a bad bout of pneumonia had Butch in and out of the hospital for three weeks, and I had some panic attacks over the thought of losing him. He's seventy-four, which isn't that old according to my parents, but Butch smoked until he turned sixty, so that hasn't done his lungs any favours.

Whenever I don't work or have an audition I go to Sunny Acres. It's got a quiet, chill vibe, with friendly staff members in cheerful scrubs. A couple of the seniors are on the batshit scale, singing loudly to themselves or randomly shouting out nonsense, but most of them are sweet and funny. I like hearing their stories and imagining them when they were young.

I pull the cord and stand while I wait for the bus to screech to a stop. The sun is shining today and helping the place live up to its happy name. I smile at the few seniors outside on the benches scattered around the lawns. One lady is in a wheelchair and hooked up to oxygen. Every so often the idea of being old myself sweeps through me, and I feel chilled up and down my spine. When this happens, I look at my unlined hands and remind myself that it's a long way from sixteen to eighty.

Inside, I pause to peer at the fish tank. It relaxes me to watch the fish swim aimlessly without worrying about anything. Not booking roles? The fish don't care. Science teacher threatening to rat out absences to Val, who will freak? No need to panic, just swim in circles all day waiting for a giant hand to drop food in your tank.

"Is that Jameson Harper? The famous actress?" I turn around to see Conrad, who is tall and bald with enormous tortoiseshell glasses. He has a tattered copy of *The Partner* by John Grisham tucked under his armpit. Butch does not approve of Conrad's reading choices, but I'll read any genre, so Conrad and I have that in common.

"It's me. No card bingo today?"

"Nope. Not on Wednesdays. We had a gardening expert in before lunch, but I got bored and read while she was talking."

We start walking toward the long hallway that leads to Butch's small room. "That's kinda rude, Conrad, to read when you have a guest speaker."

"When you get old, every minute counts."

I chuckle. He turns left when I go right to get to Butch. "Don't forget us when you're famous," Conrad calls out as I knock on Butch's pale wood door.

I hear him inside, slowly rising to his feet from his brown plaid lounge chair. He walks across the carpet in his leather moccasin slippers, flinging open the door with a bright smile on his craggy face. "There's my Ducky. Come in and take a load off."

Stepping inside, I drop my backpack on the floor and kiss his papery cheek. He smells like old Brut aftershave and leftover nicotine from a decade back. I want to bottle that smell and keep it forever. I go stretch out on his bed. "God, it feels good to lie down. School seemed extra long today." I sit up sharply. "Oh, I have amazing news for you."

He walks to my side and smiles down at me. "Let's have it."

I pause for dramatic effect, then fling my arms wide and shout, "I have a callback for a part on a new TV show!"

Butch grasps his cheeks, *Home Alone* style, in an exaggerated gesture of wonder. He performs a mini version of the electric slide near his bed, boogying to the best of his ability with an arthritic hip.

I roll off the bed and dance with him for a few seconds, until we both bust up laughing. "It's on Friday afternoon. I can get myself there, but the problem comes if I get the part. I'll need someone to stay the whole time as my chaperone. Ed is working and of course Val refuses, for stupid reasons that I'll never understand."

Butch looks at me, resisting the bait. He's heard me bitch about his daughter for the last year and a half, since I started pursuing acting. Butch tries to be fair while still supporting me the best he can. He's an excellent listener. "Any chance you can do it? I'll get a cool trailer and you'll just have to hang out and eat free food on set. Kind of like you did for that student film last year, but this is going to be a much more impressive operation."

He tips his head. "Sure, Duck Face. I'll have to check my schedule, but I think I can squeeze it in."

I throw my arms around Butch's neck and then realize my phone is buzzing in my pocket. Disentangling myself, I look at the display to see Sam's name and picture. Sam never calls. What if she's going to tell me the callback's off?

Carefully, I tap the green button and raise the phone to my ear. "Sam? Is everything okay?"

"Better than okay, Jamesy. In addition to your callback Friday afternoon, I've just booked you an audition for a feature on Friday morning. Can you go?"

"Hell yes, I can go. Thank you!" A feature film. The grin I give Butch reaches all the way to my toes.

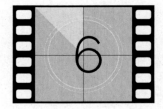

"Try not to hit the flowers, Dylan."

"Watch this!" Dylan pulls the neon-yellow foam ball toward him with his hooked right foot, bent inwards like a half-circle. He contorts his body in the opposite direction to grab the ball in his curled left hand. He tosses it in the direction of the toy plastic basketball net at the bottom of the townhouse front door stairs. The ball misses, so I drag myself up from the stair I'm sitting on and gently kick it back so Dylan can reach it.

I've been babysitting Dylan for the last year. He's a smart and stubborn five-year-old, and he lives eight doors down from my townhouse, so the commute is a breeze. He was born with his limbs all different sizes. One arm is longer than the other. His legs are bent and his feet can't bear his weight. Dylan shuffles himself around with a type of commando crawl. He uses a wheelchair at school, and he has a walker that he straps into and then paddles his feet on the ground when he wants to move around the complex and play with the other little kids.

"So close! Keep trying. Every basketball player has to practice a long time to get good." He throws it again and it falls into his mom's pink tulips. I frown at Dylan with exaggerated menace, and he giggles while readying himself for me to toss the ball back to him. I feel my phone buzz and pull it out of my jeans, hoping it's not Val and simultaneously trying to override the dart of hope surging through my veins that even more amazing acting news might be on the horizon.

> Hey buddy I'm bored should we watch a movie
> at my place instead of at work lmk

Cole. I can feel my face flush with pleasure.

"Hey guys, wanna play basketball with me?" Two young boys cruise by on scooters, and Dylan waves the ball at them. I look up from my phone and silently will them to stop and come over. One of the boys is shy and kind. He stops, lays his scooter on the ground next to the steps I'm leaning against, and walks up to Dylan.

"Okay, I'll play." Dylan tries his best to throw the ball at the newcomer, but he has to bend at the waist to be able to catch it, due to Dylan's short arm.

"This is my babysitter, Jamesy." Dylan says this with so much pride. I smile at the boy and start typing a response to Cole while keeping an eye on the other kid. He's still standing on his scooter, but narrowing his eyes at Dylan. I've seen this play out before, and it's usually ugly.

> Sorry to hear you're bored. Yes, we should watch a movie but agreeing on one could be

"What's a matter with your arms and legs?"

I glare at the boy, tall with four stringy limbs, so assured on his silver scooter. My body tenses up, but Dylan's mom says I should let him handle these altercations unless he starts to get upset.

"My arms and legs is different sizes. But I'm having a operation soon and my doctor says when I grow bigger they'll be just like everyone else's."

(Take that, you brat.) My affection for Dylan swells, and I watch him shove the ball with his bare foot to the non-asshole child playing with him. The mouthy boy across the street snorts and says under his breath, "Prob'ly not."

I step forward and raise my voice. "If everyone was exactly the same it would be a very boring world. The important thing is not to be incredibly rude." I stare the little shit down, daring him to say more, but the decade of years I've got on him wins out and he drops his eyes. In the next second he's gone, pushing hard with his back leg and gliding away on his scooter.

Dylan's busy with the neighbour boy, who remains behind to throw baskets, so I return to my text.

difficult. *Pretty Woman? Mean Girls? Les Miz?* ☺
Tell me when and where.

I'm done babysitting around seven. Maybe Cole will run lines with me for Friday's callback and the new feature audition. He wants to chill. With me. At his house.

This is officially the best week of my life to this point.

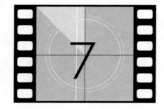

As I'm about to ring Cole's doorbell, I feel overwhelmed by a case of nerves. It could also be hunger, as I missed dinner, but I did gun a granola bar in the bus to be on the safe side. I inhale deliberately, remembering Mrs. Wu's brilliant advice to breathe our way through all panic attacks, screwed-up lines, or pages of dialogue to memorize in a brief window of time. (Okay, Jameson. You can do this.)

My hand is approaching the doorbell when the door swings open to reveal Cole. He's in navy shorts, a blue striped T-shirt, and a zippered hoodie. His mouth turns up at the corners enough to show off a faint impression of his dimples. My heart skips about three of its usual functions.

"Were you standing there waiting for me?"

"Yes. I always hover around the door. Don't you?"

I burst out laughing. Oh God. I thought I could be cool with the casual vibe I'm aiming to exude, but I have to accept that I'm crushing hard over here. Perhaps it's useless even to try. He must like me enough to invite me over, so I'll have to cling to that. Thankfully, Cole laughs too. He opens the door wider and makes a sweeping gesture with his arm for me to come in.

Walking into new houses is a visceral thing for me. Maybe it's because I love to perform, and this is part of creating a character, but where people live is fascinating. First, the smell. This house smells like pasta, garlic, cheese, apples, and something pleasantly floral, like lilacs. It's a small rancher, decorated sparsely with lots of white and few knickknacks. I love a minimalist look, so my eyes are darting around like a weirdo, trying to take it all in.

"Have you eaten dinner?" Cole puts his hand out to take my

backpack. He sets it on the floor by my shoes as gently as one would handle a baby or a kitten.

"Does a granola bar count?"

"Most definitely not." This voice is a new one, feminine, floating nearby, but I can't see who it belongs to from the entryway.

"There's nothing my mom likes more than feeding people." Cole walks up two tiled steps and I follow him into the kitchen. His mom is washing dishes, her reddish-brown hair pulled back into a high ponytail. She has a rounded frame, like I do, so I immediately feel more relaxed. (Jamesy, stop comparing your body to everyone else's and measuring if you're thinner or fatter. Try to just be comfortable and happy without aiming to be skin and bones like so many female actors. Confidence, Jamesy. Jesus.)

She turns around and grins. Wow, a lady version of Cole. "I'm Teresa. Everyone calls me Tess, but I think Teresa sounds more grown-up so I use it when I meet new people."

"Teresa it is, then. I'm Jameson, but everyone calls me Jamesy, and I don't mind because it sounds breezier, and I like people to think I'm easygoing."

"You're not?"

I shrug and turn to Cole. "What do you think?"

"Definitely not. High maintenance, but it's more fun that way." Hot damn! I can't wait to tell Lawrence he said that, and in front of his MOM.

Teresa drops the dishcloth into the soapy sink and goes to a cupboard to remove a flowered plate. "We just finished eating lasagna. I'm going to dish you up some unless you stop me."

I open my mouth exaggeratedly, then firmly close it and grin at her. Cole ambles to the fridge and grabs two cans of iced tea. He tosses one to me, then opens his and sits at the table. "Did I mention Jamesy is an actress?"

"Actor," I correct him. "No need to differentiate between genders if other jobs don't do it." I go sit beside him. Our legs are mere inches apart and now it's all I'm thinking about.

"Oh, and she's a raging feminist, like you," Cole says to Teresa.

"Wouldn't have it any other way," she responds, placing a plastic shield over my lasagna before heating it up in the microwave. "Are you graduating this year too, Jamesy?"

Cole and I exchange a glance. "No. I'm in grade ten."

"Cole! Seriously?"

"But I'm a mature grade ten! I'm on the honour roll, I work at the Lantern, I have an agent and I go on lots of auditions, I've been in school plays, I text in full sentences, I take the bus everywhere and don't rely on my parents, as they both work. I'm not a young sixteen—I promise."

Teresa is not convinced. She looks from me to Cole, who has a mock innocent expression on his face. "Hmm," she mutters as she takes my lasagna out and brings it over to me, grabbing a fork on the way to the table. "At least you are fake breezy."

"I do have that going for me." I take my first forkful of lasagna. It's amazing, with gooey mozzarella hanging from my fork to my plate. It tastes like summer vacation. I fall a little bit in love with Teresa.

"Jamesy has a callback for a TV show role on Friday. I said I'd run lines with her tonight." Cole leans over and pinches a piece of rogue noodle from my plate. (Oh God, now his leg is touching mine. That's not accidental, right?!)

Teresa swats at his hand, then returns to her sink of dirty dishes. "That's exciting! I was an actor myself back in the day. I love it when people go for the hard stuff, even if the odds are stacked against you."

I carefully swallow my bite of lasagna and wash it down with iced tea. I shift slightly in my vinyl kitchen chair so he knows my leg is right there. I feel a shiver throughout my torso at how close he is to me, then turn to face Teresa. "Thank you for saying that. Really. My mom is not happy about me acting. She wants me to pursue something more stable, like business or science, but there's no sure thing in this life, so you may as well go for what you want."

"Well said. If you keep at it with school I'm sure it will all work out."

When I turn back to my lasagna, Cole is watching me. I give him a tiny smile, then continue eating my pasta. I try to remember to breathe, because it seems my lungs have frozen up. This kitchen reminds me of my drama classroom. When I was little, trying to fall asleep, I used to dream that home could feel like this. Warm, safe, relaxed, even welcoming. For a moment, I allow something in the neighbourhood of contentment to cover me like a blanket.

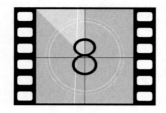

INT. CASTING OFFICE — DAY

JAMESON HARPER as LILAH (16) stands in front
of a camera, a deep frown on her face.

> LILAH
> Just wait and see what we are gonna do
> to you. This is only the beginning.
> (smiles)
> Don't push me.

Lilah crosses her arms over her chest. She
turns her head to look at MACKENZIE (16).

> MACKENZIE
> Should've stayed homeschooled, bitch!

> LILAH
> You've been warned. Officially.
> (bright)
> Come on, girls, we're late for Social
> Justice club…

The CASTING DIRECTOR (40s) laughs.

CASTING DIRECTOR
Let's stop there.
(beat)
We'll be in touch. Thanks for coming in.
Jamesy smiles and leaves the room.

⇥ ⇤

I sip my vanilla iced latte on a trendy coffee shop patio while idly scrolling through Broadway actors on Instagram. I still feel warm from the feature film audition, not to mention the sun peeking from behind the clouds to shine on me. Val has texted three times to ask why she got a call from Ms. Kuntz about my science absences this week. I stayed up late last night answering textbook questions and emailing them so I would have them done ahead of today's class, but Ms. K. has it out for me. I already have Val on my ass about auditions, and she really won't cope well if she knows how much school I actually do miss. I've been able to make it all work with my trademark bluster and charm (plus some faked calls to the office from "Val" to excuse my absences), but it's wearing thin and I can't afford to lose any teacher and parent goodwill when I'm about to miss more days if I should book the *Code Breakers* part.

> Wish me luck, buddy. My *Code Breakers* call back is at 1:15. Thanks for running lines with me. And for agreeing to *Jurassic Park*. Let's do it again soon.

I type xo and then quickly erase it. Feels too soon. I hit send, noticing that I'm not breathing, waiting for Cole to respond. Whenever I think about him (which, let's face it, is ALL.THE. TIME.), I get a version of the Nike swoosh in my belly. I'm woozy to the point of fainting. Is this what love is? How do people function in this strange state? No text bubbles appear. He must be in a No Phone class.

I finish my latte and pull my callback script toward me. Time to get the mean-girl feature role out of my head and pivot back to my character Gemma Beekdal's mad safe-cracking skills for my first official callback. This would be even more fun if someone were here with me. A person who gave a shit and was invested in my career, so I didn't have to fight so hard all by myself. If Brooklyn and I had stayed friends, we could be here together, running lines and giggling over stupid things like we used to in grade seven. Or if Butch were healthier, he could be here, reminding me that I'm not completely alone. Or Edward, if he didn't work every damn hour of the day. Or Val, if she cared more about me than what people think about her as a mother. I've even considered asking Grace to drive me to auditions, but it seems like too much to ask from my boss.

I pull my phone onto my script and text Lawrence.

> It's Friday. What are you really going to miss at school if you come into the city? It will be fun. I'll buy you food. I need you to hold my hand if I bomb the CB. Please???

Nothing. Then, when I've given up hope, this appears.

> What fucking bus do I take and exactly what food will you buy me

INT. CASTING OFFICE — DAY

Jameson Harper as Gemma Beekdal (16) crouches low, pretending to open a safe. KEN (18) stands beside her.

                    KEN
    You have to go faster than this, Beekdal.

                    BEEKDAL
    I don't see you doing anything.

                    KEN
    I'm watching the door!

                    BEEKDAL
    Yeah.

                    (beat)
    That's the most important part of this
    job.

Beekdal stands and hands Ken an imaginary
screwdriver.

                    BEEKDAL (CONT'D)
    Done. Any other notes?
                    (off his face)
    How's that door looking?

The Casting Director (35), DIRECTOR (50) and
PRODUCER (40) laugh.

                    DIRECTOR
    That was great. Now let's get Franny in
    here for the next scene.
    Jamesy nods and stretches her neck from side to side, getting
ready.

    Lawrence is sitting in the waiting room when I walk out of the
casting office. He's got his headphones on, watching something
on his phone. I'm so happy to see him. I feel like I'm floating.
He looks up, notices me, and pulls off his headphones.
    "So?"
    "So." Then I grin. He pops to his feet and gives me a bear hug.
I don't want to say too much in the waiting room filled with
other auditioning callback hopefuls like me. But way down to
my toes I know that I've given the best performance I'm capable
of in that room. If they don't pick me, someone was better suited
to the part, but right now I can't even imagine this happening. I
stepped up to bat and I swung hard. That's all I can ever hope to
do. I shouldn't be using baseball metaphors because I don't play
sports and therefore don't really grasp the subject matter. But it's

in the neighbourhood of how I feel right now.

I step away from Lawrence and lean over the coffee table to sign out. "Good luck!" I say to the rest of the room before threading my arm through Lawrence's and walking us down the stairs and out of the building. I know it's bad luck to say this to actors, but I don't exactly want any of them to get my part.

"Thanks for coming, Larry Boy. Really. I nailed it in there and I can't wait to celebrate with you. Tex Mex?"

"Fuck yeah. Let's murder a big mess of burritos and toast to you becoming a big star and buying me a ludicrous sports car so I can try to prove something to everyone."

The crowds on the street seem friendly and happy in the sunshine. It's Friday afternoon, I'm with Lawrence, and I'm inches away from the thing I want most in this world.

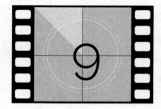

I roll over, cocooned in my marigold-yellow duvet, and slowly become aware that either Crockett or Tubbs is purring right near my head. I attempt to ignore this pleasant distraction and keep my eyes squeezed shut. The next sound is harder to ignore. It's Timmy, far too close, clearing his throat in an exaggerated manner.

"Are you awake?" he whispers, about two inches from my ear.

I stay quiet, a game of chicken that I've played many times before, but now Crockett is forcing her face into mine, so I know the jig is up.

"No," I answer, while petting Crockett with just my middle finger. Tim chuckles, as I knew he would, and jumps onto me.

"I knew you were awake." He wriggles his way under my blanket. "Mom says it's time for you to get up and do your dusting."

I sigh, forcing my eyes open. Tim smells like underarm sweat and greasy hair. He avoids showering until Val or Edward gets too close and inhales a whiff of his gross eleven-year-old self. Tim's in his weekend uniform of saggy boxer-briefs (today's feature a chimpanzee wearing sunglasses, but it's entirely possible these are from Friday or even Thursday) and nothing else. His blue eyes are looking at me under his mop of red hair. "It's eleven o'clock."

"That's early. You should've let me sleep longer." I stretch and sit up. "Did you bring my phone up?" Val makes the whole family charge our phones in the kitchen at some expensive docking station she bought. She reads articles about how bad it is to have your phone in your room at night but I'm the only one of my friends who has this restriction on my civil liberties.

"Nope. Get it yourself." Tim grabs the shoulder of my *Hamilton* T-shirt. "Stay here, James. Play with me."

I'm up and out of bed. "Can't right now. I have to see if Sam's heard anything from yesterday. Your sister could be on TV very soon, you know."

He shrugs. He's clearly thinking, "Who cares?" If I ever make it to famous, Tim will be sure to keep me level-headed and not full of myself. I love this about him.

I leave Tim in my room, stinking up the place and cuddling with Crockett, while I run lightly down the stairs in search of my phone. Edward is frying bacon along with an omelette. "Oh, so you are alive!" he says, trying to swat me with his shiny plastic flipper.

I dart past him, unscathed, and check my phone. Nothing from Sam. One text from Lawrence seeking additional grift for coming to my callback yesterday. And a surprise text from Brooklyn.

Hi Jamesy. Wanna hang out this weekend? ttyl

(What the shit? How does Brooklyn think she can dump me when we get to high school in order to upgrade to more popular friends, and then expect I'll come running like a loyal lapdog when she crooks her finger at me?) No thanks. I delete her text and sigh.

"Bad news?"

I lower my phone and look up at Edward. "No news."

Val bustles out of the small bathroom by the front door, wearing yellow rubber gloves and brandishing a half-full bottle of window cleaner. "Oh good, you're up. How did you sleep? Grab a dusting cloth and get going so your father can vacuum. Timmy did his housework hours ago."

I bite back my immediate response ("Well, isn't Tim the golden child?") and decide silence is the best option here. Edward is dishing up his grim omelette, stuffed with peppers and onions, so I plug my nose and reach around him to pull a dusting cloth out of a drawer.

I walk to the living room, moving pictures and knickknacks to swipe at the surfaces below them. Val follows me, pointing out where I missed a section. (Breathe, Jameson. Stop imagining that the cloth in your hand is a weapon. She'll go away sooner or later.) "I hope you're not planning to miss any more school right now. I logged into that parent portal at your school and I'm not happy with your science grade. Or math. Do you need a tutor?"

Edward chimes in from the kitchen around a mouthful of his breakfast, "Val, would you give her a break? She's on the honour roll. What more do you want from her?"

"How about not skipping school to go on auditions and telling her teachers we are fine with it? She may have you snowed but I see her commitment to her academics waning and we cannot allow this to happen."

Val's voice rises with each word. She turns away from me and takes a few steps to the table where Edward is likely regretting saying anything. I peer out of the living room to see him straightening the weekend edition of the sports page in front of his plate. (Good luck, Edward.) I send him the best vibes I can and duck behind Val to run up the stairs to find Timmy. He'll be hiding out, stressed, hoping this fight is short and doesn't involve him. Luckily for him, I'm the source of most of these arguments. We'll ride this out together, and if it gets really bad I'll take him to the café up the street for a hot chocolate and a peanut butter caramel pretzel cookie.

Monday, April 30th

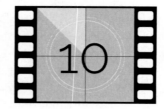

"Jamesy, why don't you come and join us? We've got space over here for you." (Oh really. How generous! It's a grade ten P.E. class in public school. I'm pretty damn certain there's room for all of us.)

I wipe the sweat off my forehead and glance at Brooklyn and her plastic-looking friends. She smiles at me, like she's hosting a TV show, and I wonder yet again what the fuck is up with her. Lawrence said he heard from Rajinder that Brooklyn bombed at her last commercial shoot. She was supposed to chug an energy drink and she kept gagging on it. The devilish side of me desperately wants this to be true, but rumours aren't always to be trusted with the high school crowd. Brooklyn asking me to hang out is strange, however, and now beckoning me over for dodgeball (the world's most humiliating and awful "sport") is extra weird. I'm not prepared to give in that easily.

"Sorry, ladies. I've got cramps and need to go take some painkillers." I walk past them and make an elaborate gesture of doubling over to my female twenty-something P.E. teacher. She makes a sympathetic face and nods as I head into the change room. Screw dodgeball. My period was last week but no one needs (or wants) this information.

I pull my phone out of my bag and hear a loud rushing sound in my ears as I stare at the screen.

> Congrats Jamesy! You booked the *Code Breakers* part! I'll email wardrobe fitting deets when I get them. Keep May 5 to 9 open for now to shoot. Fabulous job, you!!!

It's not possible for me to contain the joy spreading through my body like a virus. I run in circles around the empty change room, bananas-style, pumping my fists in the air and kicking out my legs at random. This is it. Thirty-seven auditions, every one ending in a "no," to get to this one super sweet and satisfying "yes."

The whistle blows out in the gym and I hear them lining up for another game, voices mingling and rising and trash-talking. It's not hard to tune them all out. Everything feels different for me now, like I've gone up a level, and yet no one else knows about it except for me and Sam (and the casting director, producer, director, and assistants at *Code Breakers*—bless each and every one of them for turning their light in my direction this time).

I have to tell someone. I dial Butch. It rings twice and then his scratchy voice answers.

"Butch. Guess what? You'll never guess so I'll just tell you." I pause, for dramatic effect, then shout, "I booked the part on the TV show! I go for a wardrobe fitting soon and it shoots in early May!"

"Oh Duck, I'm thrilled for you. Way to go. Aren't you at school?"

"Yeah, I'm here. Hiding out from dodgeball in the change room. The bell will ring soon for lunch. You can still take me to *Code Breakers*, can't you?"

"I'm planning on it, but…" he trails off for a moment, like he's lowered the phone, and I hear someone call his name in the distance.

"Butch? Where are you?"

"Jameson, I'll call you back later. I'm at the emergency room getting a mystery bump tested on my leg and they're ready for me now. Don't worry, I'll be fine. Thanks for calling me but go back to your class now. Just because you're a TV star doesn't mean you can skip."

"What bump? What are you talking about?"

"I have to go. Don't worry." He hangs up and I'm left staring at the phone in my hand. Why isn't he at his regular doctor's office instead of the ER? That effervescent feeling dissipates, like helium from a balloon, and I sink back to earth as the bell rings to end gym.

→ ←

Lawrence isn't at our usual lunch table so I go outside in search of him. It's misty out, and the ground is wet, but the drizzle is holding off for the moment. I weave through the outside courtyard, with its motley assortment of high school archetypes, and eventually find Lawrence alone, sitting on his torn Depeche Mode sweatshirt under a tree.

"It's wet out here! Why aren't you inside?"

I realize that he's not eating. He's staring off into the distance. At the sound of my voice, he looks up and my stomach dives south. Lawrence's face is pinched, his skin pale. His dark brown eyes are tinged red. He bites his lip and doesn't speak. Clearly, my acting news is going to wait.

I crouch beside Lawrence, my backpack in my lap. "What happened?" I ask softly.

After what feels like forever, Lawrence answers, "My dad ran some fucking program on my laptop last night while I was asleep. I always clear my browser history but he still found some stuff that he didn't want to see."

"Like what?"

He appears anguished. His voice is so quiet I have to lean forward to hear him. "Gay stuff. I was just messing around and it's not that hard-core but he freaked and is talking about military school to straighten me out."

"Oh God, Lawrence, I'm so sorry. That's awful. Give him some time and he'll settle down."

"No, he won't. Having a maybe queer son is a failure for him. A girlfriend is the only option really open to me." He sounds utterly wrecked.

I've always assumed Lawrence is gay, but it's not the kind of thing I feel comfortable asking about because it seems like he doesn't really know yet. I figure he'll tell me when he's ready. We just sort of talk around it. His parents are religious and quite conservative, his dad in particular. I usually feel nervous and fidgety around him, trying to think up excuses to get out of the room and away from his cold stare. Lawrence is sweet and gentle and funny. Who cares if he's attracted to guys? Why be such a hard-ass about it when you're supposed to love your kid unconditionally?

I sit down beside him, wet grass be damned. I can't think of anything to say that will help, but we sit together in silence until the end of lunch.

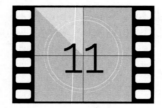

We're at the local pub for dinner. It's odd, on a Monday night, but Val came home upset over some parent bitching at her about their four-year-old who can't tie his own shoes or some such nonsense (Val's a preschool teacher—those poor kids), and when Edward walked in the door he announced, "Mom's not cooking tonight. I'm taking us all out to the pub for wings!" Edward's trying hard to be a hero. I sort of admire the effort but it also feels quite sad and desperate.

Tim considers dry garlic ribs to be the highest level of fancy cuisine, so he's chowing down over a red plastic basket of them. Val picks at her salad and Edward's hands and mouth are smeared with barbeque sauce from his wings. I ordered a mushroom burger, but after two bites I'm feeling queasy because I have to break the news about booking the *Code Breakers* part. It's going to be as messy as Edward's face.

No one is making conversation. Tim's face looks strained. (Sorry, kid, it's not going to get any better.) Time to go for it. I draw a long breath, straighten my shoulders, and paste a smile on my features. "So I have some good news." Val lowers her fork and eyes me warily. Edward, always one to keep up the front of forced cheer, says, "Oh yeah? Lay it on us."

"I booked my first TV show part. The callback was Friday and my agent told me this morning that the role is mine. It's small—only eight lines—but I'm also in two scenes where I don't have any dialogue. I'll go for a wardrobe fitting soon, and Butch says he'll go with me on set as my chaperone, so neither of you has to do anything." I know I'm rambling, but I can't seem to stop myself. "I've been working toward this for a year, and I couldn't be happier about it."

The table is quiet when I finish. Tim gives me a tiny smile but doesn't say anything. Ed reaches under the table and squeezes my knee. I toy with a yam fry and intentionally avoid Val. "Oh, Tim, my agent says my character ends up dead. I think she gets shot but I haven't seen the whole script yet, only my audition sides. My character's name is Beekdal and she breaks into safes."

"Cool," Tim says.

When I can't take it anymore, I glance at Val. Her face looks washed-out. She toys with her piece of garlic bread but has stopped eating. I guess one of her worst fears has come true. (Well too bad, Val. This is what I want most, and I've finally beaten out every other actor who auditioned for this role. It's a big accomplishment, and I'm not going to let you ruin this for me.)

I jut out my chin and look squarely at her. "What's going on with Butch? I called him this morning and he was at the hospital getting some kind of lump checked. Do you know anything about this? Is it serious?" Tim turns his head to me, alarmed.

"Of course it's not serious," Val states without making any eye contact. "It's a routine thing. Nothing to worry about. Just focus on school and everything will be fine."

I stand up, my legs trembling as much as my voice. "Oh right, you think I'm four instead of sixteen. It's obvious you don't care about Butch any more than you care about me. I'll be fine. Nothing to worry about."

I grab my bag with my wallet and phone and turn to walk out of the pub. I refuse to cry, even though tears are pushing their way into my eyes. I get outside, into the warm spring evening, and go to lean against Edward's dark blue SUV. (Screw you, Val, and Edward too, for timidly squeezing my knee to show your support but being too afraid to say anything in front of Tim or Val. Why is this so fucking hard for you? I'm doing it all on my own anyway. Would it kill you both to say "Congrats" and then carry on with your lives?)

After a series of short breaths I feel marginally calmer. I grab my phone and text Lawrence.

> How's it going at home? I'm out for the dinner
> from hell with Ed and Val. Thinking about you.
> Text me and tell me you're okay. xoxoxo

I wait, staring at the screen, but no bubbles appear. I'm staring at my phone, willing Lawrence to tell me that his dad has eased up on him, when Brooklyn's grinning face appears asking to FaceTime. I push away from Ed's vehicle, shocked, and start punching at the screen so the people going in and out of the pub don't hear my loud ringtone, when suddenly her expertly made-up face and sleek black hair fill my phone screen.

"Hey Jamesy!" She's waving as if an ocean separates us instead of a few city blocks. "I hope I'm not bothering you but I wanted to talk about how rough it is for us actors and so few people understand what we go through. My last day on set was weeks ago and there's not a lot of auditions for our age group right now. Are you as frustrated as I am?"

I can't stop staring at her perfect eyebrows, her shimmery gold highlighter, her liquid eyeliner curved up to make her eyes look bigger, and her creamy unblemished skin. I try to avoid my tiny picture at the top of the screen because my hair looks messy and I'm not wearing any makeup. I'm trying to be confident in who I am without spending hours getting dolled up but suddenly I feel insecure, dumpy, and downright ugly compared to Brooklyn. Is she sitting at home all made up like this? (Don't let it bother you, Jamesy.) Too damn late. I'm bothered.

"I can't talk right now. We're out for dinner and my family will be here soon."

"Oh, sorry about that. I'd love to hang out and talk shop with you some time."

I narrow my eyes a bit at her. "I've got a lot going on but I'll see you at school. I'm not actually finding it that quiet for auditions right now. See you later." I hit the red end button and can't resist a small chuckle.

My good humour lasts until I see Val, Edward, and Tim walking out of the pub toward me. Maybe something changed while I've been outside. Maybe it's going to be better.

Val unlocks the driver's door with the key fob and swings it open. "Let's get home. I've got lots of prep to do for tomorrow's class, and I'm sure you've both got homework."

Nope. Nothing's changed.

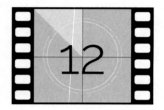

Grace sets another box down with a thump on the glass countertop. "That ought to keep you two out of trouble for a while," she says to Cole and me with a theatrical wink. "I've got bills to pay in the back. Unless one of you wants to switch with me?"

"Not it!" Cole grabs the box cutter and slices the top box, revealing rows and rows of shiny chocolate bars.

"I'd do it Grace, but I have a medical condition where the only person I know how to pay is named Jameson Harper."

She smiles at me. "Fine. You restock the candy and I'll handle the finances." Grace grabs a Coffee Crisp from the top of the box and scampers out of the lobby like a naughty toddler. Cole and I laugh.

"Want a refill?" he asks, holding up my half-empty popcorn bag.

"Nah, I'm good." He takes his empty bag to the popcorn machine and scoops it, then squeezes a ton of butter over the top. Movie theatre perks are the best.

I pull some chocolate bars out onto the counter, organizing them in groups before stuffing handfuls into the lower part of the glass case. "Good news, buddy."

Cole pauses, his hand thrust into the red striped popcorn bag. "Seriously? Is it what I think it is?"

I grin so wide it actually hurts. "Yup. You're looking at Gemma Beekdal, a safe breaker who may or may not be killed after her eight lines of dopey dialogue on an actual television show."

He stashes his popcorn on the back counter and gives me a hug. Oh God. How can anyone's body feel so hard and yet so comfortable at the same time? "I'm so impressed. You're amazing.

I'm not so sure about the getting killed part though."

He steps back, and I resist the urge to move toward him and remain in that hug forever. "I'm not getting killed. Beekdal is. Remind me to explain the concept of acting to you sometime."

"You're making a mess of that case. I'll pretty it up. You hand them to me." Cole kneels on the popcorn-littered carpet, taking one bar at a time from me and carefully stacking them.

"Thanks for running lines with me last week. It helped."

"You're welcome. I'll take twenty-five percent when you get paid."

"My agent only takes fifteen!"

"Well, my contribution was more important."

A loud bang from cinema two reverberates through the lobby, shaking the glass counter.

"Bomb scene already? Only half an hour to go." Cole takes a box of Smarties from me and I hold it so there's virtually no way he can grab it without touching me. His fingers are warm and dry. I feel a tickly sensation of pleasure radiate up my arm. I pass him a Kit Kat next, manspreading my fingers again, hoping to repeat the hand-touching scenario.

"So your mom is fantastic. She's so chill and easy to talk to. I really liked her."

"Yeah. Everyone says that."

"You don't agree?" We're getting to the bottom of the box, so I start slowing down our assembly line.

Cole sits back on his heels. "It's more complicated when you're her kid. Lately she's been at me about my future." In a mimicking, nagging tone, he says, "When are you going to decide what you want to take in university? Why didn't you apply anywhere for the early deadline?" Cole follows up with, "It's too much pressure. I might not even go to grad in a couple weeks."

"What? Why not?"

Cole sighs. He comes back up on his knees and finishes placing chocolate in the case. "I know this sounds stupid, Jamesy, but I'm not sure I want it to be over." He turns his head slightly to look up at me. (Oh God, please, please, please let my nose be clean as he's peering straight up it.)

"That's not stupid. I think I know what you mean." I have one chocolate bar left, an Aero, and when I pass it to him I let my hand linger on his. Without a word, he curves his wrist up and tightens his fingers around mine. We hold eye contact but don't speak, which is fine because my mouth has gone bone dry and my heart is beating aggressively at the base of my throat.

There's a noise from cinema two as the door closes behind an old bald guy who shuffles toward us with an empty popcorn bag. Cole releases my hand and slides his away. I smile at the old man and reach for his bag. Honestly, who gets a popcorn refill twenty minutes before the movie ends? (Dammit, chump, you're interrupting a significant life moment for me out here!)

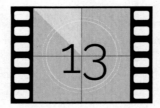

"You can talk to me. I'm right here."

"What's there to say, really. I'll just depress you."

"Try me. I can take it." The bus hits a pothole and we all feel the shudder in our bones. I'm crammed with Lawrence on the blue vinyl seat like we're kindergartners instead of teenagers. I loathe the school bus but this year I got assigned decent times, last on and first off, so I usually take it, as the city bus stop is a longer walk from school and I spend enough time on the city bus anyway. The low-grade hum of noise is constant and irritating, but thankfully our bus driver rocks this year. He's in his sixties and possesses a low tolerance for assholery. Occasionally he calls out tour guide information to a bunch of uninterested kids. Last week he announced, "Look, everyone, construction will be starting soon on that old overpass!" Good ole Terry.

I try again with Lawrence. "Is your dad talking to you at least?"

He lets out a long, frustrated breath and shakes his head. "He talks around me, like I'm so disappointing it's better not to acknowledge me at all."

"What about your mom?"

"She's making an attempt at being nice, but mostly she tries to keep the peace. My parents take the whole 'the husband's the head of the home' bullshit seriously, so his opinion is the one that matters and he's furious at the idea that I might not be 'normal.'"

"Come on, Larry Boy, no one would ever call you normal." My tone is jokey, but he doesn't smile. "Show me the fabulous outfit you're going to change into when we get to school." I lean over and start to reach into his bag, a marvelous vintage leather satchel he bought for a dollar at a garage sale at Sunny Acres right before we started high school, but he covers it with his body and turns toward the window.

"What's the point? I may as well wear this fucking prep school trash if it makes my dad happy." Okay, now I'm sinking into Lawrence's gloom. He's wearing khakis and a button-down shirt. He looks like he's heading to work as a bank teller. We spend so much goddamn time at school learning useless shit. What I want to know is when to push someone to talk and when to leave them alone. It's impossible to know what to do here.

I face forward and think for a second, hoping something inspiring and magical will occur to me, when I feel a tap on my shoulder. I turn my head to see Brooklyn. She looks like she spent three hours getting ready this morning to come to school. No one should appear that flawless. I don't buy it for a second. "I'm just wondering if you heard anything back on *Code Breakers*. They sure are taking their time on the callbacks. Has your agent said anything?"

For a moment, I consider taking the high road. But suddenly my memory takes me back to the first day of grade eight. We're at a barbeque lunch after our morning of orientation—almost four hundred new high school students outside in the September sun, nervously excited, standing around in groups from our old elementary schools. Brooklyn is giggling with some new girls, beautiful ones I've never seen before. When I approach, Brooklyn angles herself away from me and says loudly, "Isn't it amazing to be able to make new friends instead of feeling like you have to stick with the old ones from when you were a little kid?" I stop as if danger is imminent, and walk across the pavement to a group of kids I know from elementary but don't particularly like.

The bus pulls up in front of our school. I stand and glance over my shoulder at Brooklyn. "I booked that part on *Code Breakers*. It happened last week, so you can stop waiting for a callback." She looks shocked. Her perfect face clouds up and she's struggling to come up with something to say. She's saved by the throng of students pushing forward to escape the bus.

I hurry forward into the school, losing Lawrence in the process, but I need a moment to myself to savour this small victory. I planned to stay quiet and be the bigger person, but I just couldn't do it. My phone vibrates, and I peel off from the crowd to lean against a locker and read the screen. It's Sam.

> *Code Breakers* wardrobe fitting at Imperial Studios Thurs at 3. Do you want to try background on a MOW this Fri? I can book you!

I can feel the loopy grin spreading across my face. Do I want to work on a TV Movie of the Week the day after my first wardrobe fitting at an actual film studio? I start typing.

> YES YES YES YES to all of it! You are the best agent on the planet and I love you to bits. THANK YOU SAM!!

"Look at this new game I got, Jamesy! You spin this wheel and if you get a six, a dragon comes to breathe fire on you." Dylan shoves a board game in the general direction of my face.

"Sounds like a blast." (Damn, I make myself laugh.) "Let's play it."

Dylan slides it onto the table and climbs up onto a chair. While he's setting it up, keeping up a running commentary about each character in this bizarre game, I tap out a text on my phone under the scratched pine table.

> How's that messed up leg? Does it hurt? Can you still come with me next week for the TV show? I need you, Butch! ☺☺

I watch Dylan wildly spin the wheel and move his Giant character by pushing it with the palm of his hand. "I hate math," he tells me, with no context or lead-up whatsoever.

"So many of us do," I say sympathetically while opening my texts to Lawrence.

> I'm babysitting. Where are you? Care to distract me with some 80s trivia? I'm waiting...

No response from Larry Boy.

I try to concentrate on Dylan's instructions for my turn, but I'm hopelessly confused. I spin the wheel and slide my Elf character ahead when I get a three. "Soon you'll be at the dragon's lair!" Dylan informs me.

We are interrupted by a key in the lock at the front door. "Sounds like your mom's home." Dylan starts to complain about how we just started to play, but I jump to my feet.

"Sorry about that but it's time for me to go home. We'll play next time. Want me to help you clean this up?"

"No, I'll wait for Dad to get home. Mom hates this game." I don't blame her.

"Hi guys," Elise calls up the stairs. I ruffle Dylan's hair and whisper, "Hope you roll lots of sixes" in his ear. I run down the stairs and slide my feet into my Keds while pocketing the twenty Elise hands to me.

"Thanks, Jamesy. Have a good night."

I walk out the front door into the calm spring evening and make the short walk home. As I climb the front steps, I can hear Timmy complaining about something or other from our open living room window.

When I step inside, he comes running to me in his grey pirate ship boxer-briefs. "I have to hand in this book bag project tomorrow and it's sooooo hard!" Tim falls to the floor, boneless, wailing as if he's on a battlefield, shattered by unparalleled grief. This kind of thing is so common in our house that I just step over him and hang my sweatshirt on a hook. "You know what helps with book projects due tomorrow? ACTUALLY DOING THEM."

I walk into the kitchen and tense up when I see Val hunched over at the table, cutting strips of coloured cardstock with a paper trimmer. I pour myself a glass of water as Val says through clenched teeth, "I swear to God, Timothy, if you don't go upstairs right now and finish your homework you are not going to like the next words that come out of my mouth."

He wails again, banging his fists of fury against our hardwood floor, before coming to his feet and storming up the stairs. Val and I both wait, primed for the door slam, flinching only a little when it arrives. She looks at me and smiles. I can't seem to resist offering her one in return. "Parenting," she mutters while forcing a bright orange piece of paper into the trimmer. "So much fun than advertised."

"Where's Edward?"

"Working late. Of course." She stacks the orange pieces and pushes the trimmer to the centre of the table. "Come sit down. I feel like I never see you these days."

I grab an apple from the white ceramic fruit stand and bring my water to the table. I sit at the far end, giving Val lots of space with her craft supplies for her class. She fiddles around with the small shards of paper, gathering them into neat piles. (Am I supposed to talk first? She asked me to sit down!) The silence is getting awkward. Val stops messing with the paper and actually looks at me. I notice with a jolt that she's got dark circles under her eyes and the skin around her mouth looks strained and lined.

"How's school?"

(Since you asked, Val, Lawrence is depressed. Brooklyn's a bitch. My science quiz was rough and Ms. Kuntz is on me to stop missing classes to keep my A average. I'm worried about the amount of days I'll be away for *Code Breakers* and the MOW but I'm also so exhilarated I could float away from this table.) "Fine."

The silence falls again, prickly and thick. I feel dread in my body, the way I did as a kid when I heard a storm warning. "Butch says you've asked him to take you for this acting thing. He's got some doctor's appointments right now that take precedence over your creative hobbies. You assured us that your grades wouldn't fall if you kept going to auditions, but Ms. Kuntz has been in touch about your science mark, and your father and I are both very concerned. We would like you to wait before committing to any acting pursuits until you are older and can manage your time better. Right now, school must be number one. Do you hear what I'm saying to you?"

The hand holding my apple is trembling. Adrenaline courses through me. I feel the urge to run, to flee, to fling my fruit at her face and shriek like a baboon. My thoughts are swirling around like a building tornado. (Or what, Val? If I say no to your bullshit ultimatum, are you going to kick me out of the house? Disown me? What do I have left to lose if I disobey this vague and distressing statement? I've been trying for this for so long and now that it's here you want me to say no to it?!) Very slowly, I stand. I leave the apple and the water, not trusting my hands to hold them safely. Far in the distance, over our heads, I can hear Timmy crying. I say, "I heard what you said."

I walk to the stairs, forcing the tears back and holding my

head ramrod straight. Her voice sounds like staccato bullets behind me. "Jamesy. Are you going to turn down this role and focus on school as I've asked?"

I cannot turn my head. I'm a robot, programmed to walk up the stairs as far away from her as possible. Swallowing hard, I force my voice to sound as casual as I can make it under these circumstances. "I heard what you said," I repeat, before disappearing from her sight.

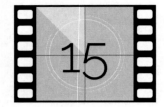

"Ooohh, let's try this one! It's got such an interesting drape and it will look stunning with that skirt." I take the hanger with the blue plaid shirt on it, long and scooped in the back and shorter in the front. I hold it up against me and dance around with it. Simone laughs, a throaty sound from deep in her chest, and shoos me away with a flick of her ring-laden hand.

I turn and head into the small dressing room behind me, pulling the brown curtain across. I've been here at Imperial Studios for the last hour, trying on one look after another, and being waited on by Simone and occasionally her boss, Richard (an older gay man in a fabulous tuxedo T-shirt that's been glitzed up with a fringe and beads, who calls me "dearest" like we're in one of Grace's beloved black-and-white films). I've successfully shut Val out of my mind, along with Lawrence, and Butch, and Brooklyn—really anyone who isn't a part of this happy moment for me. I'm soaking it up, like a plant in a soft spring rain, knowing that this is what it feels like when you are making your dream a reality.

The shirt fits well. I open the curtain and step out. Simone claps and shouts, "Yes! That will do just fine for your first scene with the safe."

Richard weaves his way through bins of labelled hats, socks, tights, mittens, and God knows what else. He's holding the same dress I'm going to wear in my death scene, but this version has fake blood all over it. Richard holds it up. "Your opinion?" he asks.

"That's literally the greatest thing I've ever seen in my life."

He grins. "Glad you approve."

Simone is busy tagging my hangers in the dressing room. "Okay, you're done with us, my darling. But I think hair and makeup want a few minutes to plan your different looks. Can you wait for them to come see you?"

"Absolutely. I can wait all day."

"You won't have to do that. It was lovely to meet you, Jamesy. Good luck as Beekdal, and I'm sure we'll cross paths again in the future!"

I draw the curtain and change out of the skirt and the plaid shirt. I feel a cozy glow spread through my torso. These are my people, in this wardrobe department. They love what they are doing and it shows. We are making a television show, dammit! The excitement is palpable.

When I emerge, Simone is writing something down on a clipboard. She gestures to a chair at the edge of the wardrobe area and I head over to it. I pass a table with the coolest jewellery on it. A lady is hunched over a bracelet, looking at it under a magnifying glass, bedazzling it with fake stones and a glue gun. People scurry to and fro, carrying clothes or props. I should be doing my science homework, but it's fascinating to watch what's going on in here. I want to live in this studio world forever.

When there's a tiny break in the action, with no one in my immediate view, I grab my phone and text Butch.

> I'm at Imperial Studios in the wardrobe department. Officially the coolest moment of my life. My work dates should be middle of next week but not sure yet. Will you be okay to come with me? How's the leg?

A guy with dreads walks past carrying an armful of wigs. He gives me a sly wink. I hope the hair and makeup people take their time so I can see even more. My phone chimes and I glance down to see Butch's response.

> I hope so. Tmrw I have to go in for a small prcdre for this leg bump. But don't worry! Cool on the studio thing. Impressive.

What procedure? Is that what he means or did he just type garbage in to irritate me? Why are some words spelled out and some abbreviated in such a goofy manner? (Come on, Butch!) Is this what Val was talking about last night? I'm wondering how to put this in a text that sounds reasonably calm, when a stunning young woman leans down in front of me with her hands on the knees of her faded ripped jeans. "You must be Jameson. I'm Suki, from makeup. We've got a table set up in the corner over here and we'd like to see what will work for your character."

"Sounds like fun." I stand up and follow her, thinking about how many times I've imagined this while trying to fall asleep, and I still can't believe it's actually happening in real time.

Thursday, May 3rd

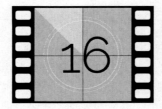

Yes, you'll need a chaperone tomorrow because it's a small # of BG and I got you on a union voucher (yay—more $!) You can't work alone until you turn 17 unless it's non-union

I stare at this text from Sam, trying to ignore the icicles of fear creeping up my spine. The bus rocks gently from side to side, pushing me into the lady beside me, who is trying to balance a bouquet of pink roses with two bags of groceries on her lap. Tomorrow I'm scheduled to do my first day of background work (BG sounds so much cooler than what it used to be called: an extra in the scene) and I have no one to go with me. Butch has his leg thing to deal with and God knows I'm not able to ask my frustrating parents. The last thing I want to do is cancel, but my mind is running around in scared circles and I can't think straight.

I look up from my phone and try to breathe. The late afternoon sun brightens the streets and makes them appear cheerful. Suddenly I realize I'm near Cole's house. I reach up and pull the stop cord.

When the bus rolls to a stop, I get off and walk to his front door. (What exactly is the plan here, Jameson? Yes, there's a fun flirty energy between you and Cole, but is it weird to ask him to skip school and pretend to be eighteen tomorrow as your chaperone so you can work on a real set? Will this draw too much attention to the fact that you're younger than he is?) I stand for a long time at the door, arguing with myself, before deciding to be brave. I raise my hand and knock.

I wait, then Teresa opens the door. "Jamesy. Hello."

"Hi. Is Cole here?"

"No. He's at Big Dave's. He's supposed to be studying but I'm sure he's playing video games."

"Oh, okay." I fidget for a second, looking down at my feet and feeling unreasonably crushed. I wish it were easier to make these puzzle pieces of life fit into place.

"Do you want to come in? I'm eating microwave popcorn and watching *New Girl*."

"Yes, please," I say in a small voice. She steps back and I walk inside.

I follow her into the living room, where Zooey Deschanel is frozen on the screen, her arms above her head and her mouth wide open like she's shouting. I sit in a leather recliner, so comfortable it's like sinking into a hotel bed. Teresa watches me with an expression of concern. "Is something wrong?" she asks.

I breathe in and out for a few moments, trying to collect myself. When I start speaking, I realize that I'm dangerously close to tears. My words come out in a tangled jumble. "It's just that I'm working tomorrow, on a movie of the week, and it's my first day on a real set as background, like being an extra, and my agent told me I need a chaperone. Next week is my first speaking role on a TV show, and my grandpa's going with me, but he can't tomorrow because he's got something wrong with his leg and he has to go to the doctor about it."

I can't hold the tears back. I wipe at my eyes and look at Zooey's mad face so I don't have to look at Teresa, who was nice to invite me in and is probably now regretting this emotional mess in her living room. "I had a wardrobe fitting today at a studio. It was so much fun. I loved every minute of it. And then on the bus my agent texted to make sure I had an adult with me tomorrow and my parents have to work, so out of desperation I thought of Cole but now I'm realizing that's stupid because he has school and he's not old enough anyway. So I have to cancel and it's ridiculously frustrating." I run my hand across my snotty nose and finally make eye contact with Teresa. She looks sympathetic and my embarrassment recedes a bit.

She stands and walks to a bookshelf in the corner of the room, grabbing a box of tissues and crossing back to my chair. Teresa hands me the box and crouches beside me. I pull a few tissues out and blow my nose. "I'm sorry to come in here and bawl like that."

"Don't apologize. It's okay. Sounds like you needed to talk to someone, and I'm glad I was here."

I draw a long, shuddering breath and stop crying. It's like I've swallowed a hit of helium. Some care and kindness really do go a long way.

"What about Grace, your boss at the movie theatre? Would she go with you?" Teresa asks.

I think about this, then say, "She's great, and really supportive about my auditions, but it feels too weird to ask her to chaperone because she's my boss. And she works so much at Lantern that I think she'd say no anyway. Film and TV means long hours, and it's unpredictable." I blow my nose one more time. "It's hopeless. I'll just have to cancel."

Teresa smiles. "Cole's been talking about you a lot lately." (Wait, what?!) "He's really impressed by how hard you've been working for what you want. He's not sure what he wants to do with his life, so he's inspired by your ambition and drive." Hot damn. My eyes hurt from crying but this piece of intel suddenly cheers me up. Teresa puts her hand on my knee and squeezes. "I don't have any meetings tomorrow. I've got a ton of emails to return and some design work to do, but it's portable. I'd love to see what a film set is like. Would I be a suitable chaperone in place of your grandpa?"

It takes a while for this to sink into my tired brain. I turn my head to see if I've imagined this. Teresa offers up a small smile.

"Seriously?" I ask.

She shrugs. "Sure. Why not? Sounds like fun."

I burst into tears once again, but this time they're hot with relief and gratitude.

Friday, May 4th

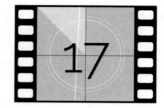

A gust of wind makes the walls of the large white tent shudder, like it's got a fever. The tent is set up on the corner of a parking lot. I'm sitting on a folding chair with the name of a party-planning company stamped on it, leaning over a long grey plastic table and trying to concentrate on my homework, but I have too much adrenaline coursing through my system to focus on math. Teresa sits across from me, dragging words and pictures around with her fancy mouse on her MacBook Pro as she works on some graphic design for a client. She's been stellar so far today in background holding, giving me space to go to and from set on my own, but being there to ask if I want to go to craft services (or crafty, for us BG pros) with her for snacks or if I needed any help filling out my union voucher this morning. Okay, rattling off these movie terms might make me sound blasé and chill, but I'm anything but. Every nerve ending is jangling. This is what it means to be alive. Before today it was just a rehearsal for what I'm meant to do with the rest of my days.

Teresa was even kind enough to drive me, at the stupid hour of five a.m., since my call time was six a.m. in downtown Vancouver. She said it was an adventure and bought me a coffee and a bacon and egg breakfast sandwich at Tim Hortons (only to arrive at holding and find a hot buffet breakfast waiting for background, cast, and crew—why in the world isn't every single person doing film work for the free food alone?!). We spent the drive mostly talking about Cole. I can tell she's concerned that he doesn't want to go to his grad and that he's procrastinating on any university applications, but she's careful to talk around these things with me. I told her that I think he'll regret not going to grad and that I plan to encourage him to go. Then she changed the subject to my future and where I might want to go to school.

Our wrangler, Mark, calls from his table at the front of the tent, "Five-minute warning for everyone in that last scene. We'll shoot the turnaround and then it will be lunch." I try not to grin, looking like a wacko, but I can't seem to grasp that I'm here, working on a romance movie of the week. The other background people start moving around the tent, preparing to head back to set. I make eye contact with Teresa and she winks at me. I spear a golden piece of pineapple from my crafty plate and pop it into my mouth, then grab my phone to text Butch.

> Butch how are you feeling? I'm on a set and everything is great but I'm worried about you. Let me know on that bum leg. I love you

Mark still hasn't called us for set so I send a text to Lawrence. He's gone silent on me, and I can tell I'm going to have to force the issue to make sure he's okay. This weekend I'm planning to show up at his house and try to see for myself what's going on with his dad.

> It's been days Larry Boy and no word from you. I need proof of life. Don't do anything scary. You're too valuable for that. Who else would school me in fine 80s culture? Seriously. Please let me know you're okay.

Mark stands and waves his arms at us. Time to go to set.

EXT. COFFEE SHOP — DAY

JAMESON HARPER (16) walks down the busy street toward the coffee shop. She opens the door and steps in.

INT. COFFEE SHOP — DAY

The two lead characters, Candace and Marty, engage in a flirty conversation at a table.

                        CANDACE
        You've never been to Paris.

                         MARTY
        No point in going to Paris until I met
        you.

        Jameson crosses in front of their table and
        stands at the counter, silently placing a
        coffee order.

                        CANDACE
        Well... what are we waiting for?

                        DIRECTOR
        Cut! Great energy.

                        FIRST A.D.
        Reset and let's go again.

        Jameson heads back outside to her first mark
        to wait for the next take.

                            → ←

            I grab a glass of iced tea from crafty and go back to holding to
        tell Teresa all about the scene (and how I was plucked from the
        crowd outside to walk into the coffee shop and be right near the
        leads!). I check my phone, hoping for a response from Butch or
        Lawrence, but no joy. There is, however, a voicemail from Val. I
        hesitate before listening to it, as I don't want anything to dull
        this sparkle I'm feeling. Maybe I should text Brooklyn instead of
        listening to Val tell me how I've disappointed her. It's tempting
        to rub this thrill in Brooklyn's face, but she considers background
        work beneath her, so it's not worth it. With a sense of foreboding,
        I lift the phone to my ear and listen to Val's tense voice. "Jameson,
        your grandfather is staying in the hospital overnight as they've

biopsied the lump in his leg and he's running a fever. I'm here, but if you can make the time in your schedule you might want to come by Pacific Hospital to see him."

Friday, May 4th

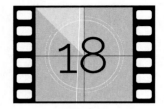

"I'm sorry, but visiting hours are over." The nurse has a marvellous square body and stands with her legs apart and her arms crossed over her enormous boobs. She has the build of a linebacker. It's nine p.m., I've been awake since four this morning, and I feel strung out and unable to handle this woman and her rules when Butch is somewhere behind her.

Teresa steps forward and helps me. "Jameson's mom is in room seventeen waiting for her to arrive to visit her grandfather. She won't be long but she really wants to see him. Isn't that worth bending the rules?"

I'm not hopeful this nurse is about to be nice to me, but from down the hall I see a flash of brown hair. Suddenly I'm weak in the knees as Cole strides toward me. Even with my hair and makeup all fancy from the set, I must appear upset, because Cole pulls me into his arms. Mmmm, I could stay here forever, except that I can sense the nurse glaring and Teresa standing next to us. He smells incredible, a combination of french fries and pleasantly spiced deodorant.

"How did you know we were here?" asks Teresa.

Cole steps back but slides his arm down mine and we interlace fingers. I feel faint for a moment, so I squeeze his hand to make sure he's really holding mine. Yup, he squeezes back. (We are actually holding hands!) "Jamesy texted me after she heard from her mom. I was at work, but Grace said I could leave as she was still there. Anyway, both movies suck this weekend so hardly anyone was there for the late show." Cole turns toward Teresa and says, "Mom, I can take over from here and drive Jamesy home when she's ready to go."

"Jamesy, are you okay?" Teresa asks. "You look pale."

I nod. "I'll be okay. Thank you, so much, for taking me today and staying with me. I owe you big time."

She waves her hand at me. "Don't be silly. I had fun too. I hope everything's okay with your grandpa."

I smile at her. She squeezes my arm and brushes a piece of fluff from Cole's pale green T-shirt. "See you at home." Teresa turns and walks down the corridor. The phone rings and the guard nurse grabs it, barking out commands. Cole pulls me away from the desk and we hurry to room seventeen.

Butch is in the hospital bed, wearing a white T-shirt and a navy robe. Val reads in a chair in the corner. She stands as we walk in. Reluctantly, I drop Cole's hand and move to Butch while Cole hangs back in the doorway.

"Duck Face," Butch says in a dry voice. "How was your first big day on a real movie set?"

"It rocked. Except that I worried the whole time about you." I sit on the edge of his bed. He reaches out a warm, papery hand to me and I take it between mine. "What exactly are you up to with this hospital stay?"

"It's just the doctors being extra cautious. When an old man runs a slight fever they seem to panic. You know I'd rather be in my own bed."

"But what about this biopsy business?"

"We have to wait for results. A stupid little spot on my leg. When it comes back negative it will all have been a fuss for nothing."

I lean against him, my head tucked under his chin like I used to do when I was small. My safe spot, I called it. I breathe deep and will myself to believe what Butch is saying. He's going to be fine. He has to be.

Val comes to my side. "I think it's time to let Butch sleep now. I'll get him settled and then drive you home."

"I can take her if you want to stay longer, Mrs. Harper," Cole pipes up from the doorway.

She turns and gives him a frosty stare. "It's no problem. I'll take her."

I sit up and sigh. Obviously, I'd rather go with Cole, but I'm not sure I want to engage Val right now, especially because I've come here straight from the set that she ordered me not to go to. I lean over and kiss Butch's smooth cheek. "I love you, Butchie. Hang in there."

He cups the side of my face, then lowers his hand. I get off the bed and go to Cole. "Val and Butch, this is Cole. I work with him at Lantern. He's terrific."

Butch smiles but Val remains closed off. I can tell she's dying to know how old he is and why he came to the hospital tonight. I step out into the hallway with Cole.

"It means a lot to me that you came. And your mom going with me today when she hardly even knows me…I can't even…" I trail off, unable to find the right words. Cole's head is leaning down and I'm swimming around in his green eyes, the colour of a smooth Rocky Mountain lake.

"I think you're pretty terrific yourself, buddy." His lips are an inch from mine. My pulse is jumping. Every beeping machine, hushed hospital voice, and squeaky rubber sole on the shiny floor fades away into silence. My whole world is Cole. Quietly, he says, "I can't stop thinking about you," and I push up on my toes so my lips graze his. It's like jumper cables to every nerve of my being, a set of fireworks in my brain saying *my first kiss* over and over in exploding light and sound. I want this moment to last forever.

"Ahem." Cole and I separate instantly, as if we've never met. Val looks at us with a shocked expression. Cole begins to back away.

"See you at work, Jamesy. Hope Butch is better soon."

I smile at him, trying to cover the shitty awkwardness of Val's unwelcome interruption. When he's gone, I stare down at my feet, replaying every second of our brief first kiss, refusing Val the satisfaction of eye contact or verbal connection. She can be the one to suggest we go home (or demand to know why I'm kissing a boy in a hospital hall, why I went to work on a MOW with Cole's mom or what my goddamn science grade is). For now, she says nothing at all and I'm glad, so I can stay lost in this incredible hazy dream just a little bit longer.

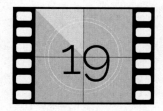

> BEEKDAL
> Look at this code! Have you
> ever seen anything so inscrutable?
>   (beat)
> Well, I'm not worried. You?

I'm sitting in bed, leaning against my wall, poring over my script for Tuesday. I swear I had this dialogue on a loop in my head as I slept last night, so I'm not worried about forgetting it, but I'm looking into the mirror trying to hit each word in a specific way. I want to slay in front of the cameras, not just deliver clunky lines. It's supposed to be funny, and goddammit, I'm going to make everyone laugh.

A firm knock sounds at my door. Has to be Edward, because Val always knocks once, then barges in. "Hi Ed."

The door opens with its trademark squeak, reminding me to oil it (which I'll promptly forget to do). Edward smiles, his hair messy from his early morning run. "Okay if I come in?"

"Sure, but keep your distance. You look grim. And sweaty."

He steps inside, dramatically swinging the door back and forth to create some air. He lifts his arm so his furry pit is exposed under his grey workout shirt. "Your father should put WD-40 on this messed-up hinge."

"Yeah, he should, but he's lazy."

"Sounds about right."

Edward leaves the door alone and starts wandering around my room, lifting a framed picture here and an old stuffed elephant there. I wait, guessing this is about Val in some way. It could also be about me kissing Cole last night—oh God, my pulse is spiking just thinking about it. I watch Edward and think about how fun he was when I was little. He'd come home from work and we'd do this elaborate game of hide-and-seek. He knew the names of all my dolls and stuffies. We spoke in a shorthand code no one else understood. It seemed like we lived in our own little world for a lot of years, and then I grew up and that easy connection with him vaporized. When he speaks now it sounds loud in my quiet room. "I was thinking it would be good for us to have a dad-daughter date like we used to. Go to Tim Hortons and I'll buy you a hot chocolate and a maple glaze. What do you say?"

"I haven't eaten a maple glaze donut in years. Raspberry jelly is where it's currently at. But what I really need are rides and chaperones to set. Not Tim Hortons."

Edward sighs, then stops fiddling around with my stuff and turns to face me. "Jamesy, you know I'd love to help you but I can't. I'm working to support this family. I'm in commissioned sales, so if I don't hustle every month, we can't pay the mortgage or our bills."

"It's not an easy thing to book a role in a TV show. I've been trying for a long time now so I know how tough it is. But I did it." I wave my script in front of him. "On Tuesday, I'm going to have my own trailer on a studio lot and I will deliver actual lines and get paid for it. And yet you still won't help me with this." I have to stop talking now as I'm close to tears. It's too raw, especially when he just blatantly lied to my face about how he'd love to help me.

"We are proud of you, really." I stare at the pattern on my duvet cover, knowing it's bullshit and hoping he'll recognize it as such if I wait this out. "But do you have to do this now? How about waiting until college, when you won't need a chaperone and you can drive yourself around and be sure this is what you want to do?"

"I am sure." The words tumble out, one running into the next. "I'm not going to wait. I just booked my first role so I can't even believe you are still asking me to stop. You and Val just don't get it." Now the tears are front and centre. Thankfully, I spot Tim hovering in the hallway with Battleship under his spindly arm.

I clear my throat and try to regain my composure by refusing to look at Edward. "Come in, Timmy. Looks like you're ready to be spanked in Battleship again."

He threads his way past Edward and jumps on my bed. "I won last time. Remember? You couldn't find my sub?"

I drop my script and reach for the box. "No way. I sunk four of your stupid boats before you hit one of mine."

Tim protests loudly. I swallow my tears. Edward walks out of the room without another word.

Saturday, May 5th

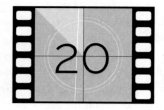

I turn the corner by the run-down market still advertising video rentals and walk down Lawrence's street. The comforting smell of lilacs reaches me a moment after I've passed the blooming bushes, the air from my body rustling the purple flowers enough to release their potent perfume into the air. I stop to inhale, trying to get to the end of my *Code Breakers* scene in my mind. But this is too good to miss. As an actor, I'm supposed to stop and notice things. Now is as good a time as any to try. The sun is warm on my back, the lilacs are calling for my attention, I'm checking to be sure Lawrence is okay before work, and I need to stop obsessing over my unsatisfactory chat with Edward this morning. At least I beat Tim in Battleship. He accused me of cheating, which is his go-to move when he loses, but I wrote a note in my phone that I won for the next time Tim's memory is fuzzy.

I start moving down the cracked sidewalk again when a woman jogs past and frowns at me. I probably look odd staring into space, but I feel refreshed by just standing still. I'm two houses away from Lawrence's when my phone buzzes. I pull it out of my back pocket. It's Cole. A whoosh of liquid joy floods through me.

> How's my fave code breaker? I can't stop thinking about you. Is Butch ok? Hurry up and get to work. It's so shitty without you

I grin to myself, picturing his soft lips brushing mine at the hospital last night. His hand resting lightly on my hip. Those green eyes closed, his dark eyelashes so close to mine. An ache that's an exquisite form of pain begins to throb in my lower abdomen. I find it challenging to breathe in and out. My lungs seem to be on pause. I love that he repeated "I can't stop thinking about you" in his text when he said it right before we kissed. I start typing.

> Going to cheer Lawrence up then I'll come to you. Butch still in hospital but okay. Happy you can't stop thinking about me because I feel the same. Last night was magic

I hit send and then worry that last bit sounded stupid. Cole is seventeen and three-quarters and I don't want to advertise that I'm only sixteen. But it *was* magic. I carry on to Lawrence's pale blue house when I see that Cole is responding. I wait for words to replace the bubbles. Please oh please, let Cole agree our kiss was magic.

> My magic wand's ready for more

Ha! I laugh to myself, glad I took the risk and didn't go for the safe route. I'm dreaming up a witty response when Lawrence's front door opens. Cole will have to wait. I tuck my phone away and smile at Jean, Lawrence's mom. She's Black and looks so much younger than Lawrence's dad. Jean is glamorous, like she belongs on a magazine cover. She's always dressed in some killer outfit with her hair and makeup done in the latest style, even though she doesn't go out to work. She volunteers on loads of committees and heads the PTA. She's friendly but formidable.

"Were you not planning to knock? I was tidying up and I saw you standing out here."

I lean over to give her a quick hug. "I was texting. Is your son home? He seems to be ignoring me so I wanted to see him before work."

Jean steps back so I can walk inside. Lawrence's house is picture-perfect. He hates it. He told me that when he moves out he's going to let an inch of dust settle on every surface and never put anything where it belongs. "Larry's in the backyard with Puddles. I just made banana muffins. Take some out to him." We walk down the hallway, papered with framed photos of Lawrence documenting him at every single age. "Michael, look who's here."

Lawrence's dad drinks coffee at the kitchen table. He's reading the Globe and Mail newspaper. I smile and offer an awkward wave. "Enjoying your Saturday?" I ask like a middle-aged person because Michael makes me nervous. He's a square white man with a crew cut. He looks like one of those marines in the movies who screams insults at new recruits while they run twenty miles in the pouring rain.

"Not bad so far. You here to be a good influence on our son?" (What in the hell am I supposed to say to that?!)

"Sure thing, Mr. Drury. Thanks for the muffins, Jean!" I grab three and open the glass patio doors as quickly as possible, closing them behind me with a sense of relief. Why oh why can't parents just be calm and normal? Why is there always such a weird atmosphere around them?

Lawrence tosses a frayed tennis ball to his brown-and-white collie Puddles. She's old and has loved me forever, so she turns her back on Lawrence and limps over to me. "Hi Puddles. You're looking beautiful today." I rub the rough fur by her ear with one hand while balancing the muffins with the other. "Lawrence. You're quite hot as well."

He drops the ball and takes a muffin from me, then shrugs. "I have to work at it but it's worth it every time I look into the mirror."

I sit on the expensive outdoor patio set and nibble at one of the muffins. It's threaded with black banana veins and packed with toasted walnuts. "Cole kissed me last night." I know my face is highlighted pink, and I don't care.

Lawrence comes to sit down next to me. "No way. You slut. And with an older dude too. Val must be thrilled."

"She actually interrupted us in the hallway at the hospital. We were visiting Butch." I laugh and Lawrence snickers. I lean over to nudge him with my shoulder. "I've been worried about you. Things better with your dad?"

"Define better. He wants the porn incident forgotten and never, ever brought up again. All he wants is the perfect hetero son, but I'm not sure I can deliver." His face looks sad.

"If he's disappointed in you, I'll give him Val's number and they can cry on each other's shoulders about what wastes of skin their kids are."

"Yeah. Getting a part in a TV show. What a miserable failure."

"I think Val would prefer me looking at gay porn." He chuckles, erasing for a second that haunted expression. "Wanna come with me to work? I want you to admire the gorgeous Cole, and Grace is playing *12 Angry Men* at four. You'll love it."

"Okay. As long as you sneak me in for free and hook me up with a large popcorn. And real butter. None of this fake marg bullshit."

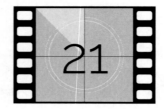

"Hey, wait for me! I'm coming too." Dylan scoots on the smooth gravel of the playground toward a group of younger kids. Usually kids Dylan's age or older won't play with him because he's not as fast as they are. I watch from the park bench, hoping I don't have to get involved. A girl about four years old with French braids turns from the pack of preschoolers to wait for Dylan. *Thank you*, I try to say to her with my expression. When Dylan catches up, they move together toward the slides. We like this park because it has a ramp for Dylan to scooch up instead of rough metal stairs, which are tough on his knees and hands when he climbs them.

I go back to running lines. I have my script tucked under my leg, but I've only had to check it once in the twenty minutes I've been sitting here. My mind keeps nosing ahead to Tuesday on the *Code Breakers* set. I wonder what kind of trailer I'll have and what it will feel like when the assistant director calls for me to come to set. When I think about it my insides are like jelly that's not quite set.

The only hang-up is Butch. I've texted him a few times this morning to see how he's doing, and I'm worried that I haven't heard back. Although, it must be said, Butch isn't exactly stellar at anything internet-related. I come to the end of my *Code Breakers* death scene in my head and scroll through Insta for a mental break. Dylan and the little kids are now playing some version of hide-and-seek, so he's okay. I'm lost in actor's posts and pictures for a few minutes when a text pops up from Butch.

> Hi Duckie. STOP worrying. I'm home from hospital. No fever.Biopsy results in a few days.

> I'll be fine and can take you Tuesday for your
> starring role.Love you. Check in with your mom,
> okay? See you soon.

I exhale with relief. Butch can chaperone and I won't have to scrabble around begging other people over the age of eighteen to help me because my own fucking parents are so unwilling to be cool.

> Thank you Butch!! You are the absolute best
> and I love you forever. Rest up and thanks!!!!

I hear female teenage voices and look over toward the trees. Oh shit, it's Brooklyn and a group of her irritating new friends. They carry huge paper coffee cups and they're nibbling on breakfast sandwiches and cake pops like rabbits. I notice that all four girls are dressed like they are going to a club in downtown Vancouver instead of walking through a neighbourhood park in White Rock on a Sunday at lunch time. I'm wearing black leggings, an old T-shirt with kittens on it, and beat-up runners. My hair is in a ponytail and I have no makeup on. One of the snottier girls waves her cup at me. I smile politely and look down at my phone. (Come on, Jameson, stop feeling so insecure. Brooklyn is the one who replaced you as her friend.) I don't have to do anything except ride this out and hope Dylan is ready to go home soon.

Out of the corner of my eye I can see a person approaching. Of course it's Brooklyn. When she's directly in front of me, in her jeans, cropped plaid shirt, and high-heeled burgundy boots, she asks, "Mind if I sit down?"

"Your friends are over by the trees."

"So you don't want me to sit down?"

"It's a free country, Brooklyn. And a public park. Sit if you want to or go back to your friends."

She sits and crosses her legs at the ankles. "It feels like I don't see you much anymore. I thought we could catch up."

That's it. I can't take more of her shit right now. The anger bubbles up and over, like a pot of water on the stove. "What is up with you? You're the one who ditched me, remember? From kindergarten to grade seven: best friends. Then grade eight comes and you acted like I caught the plague. You stopped talking to me and now you're cozying up to me again—why the hell is that, exactly? Is it because I booked a part and now you're scared I'll make it big and you don't want to be left behind?"

Brooklyn flushes red, her coffee trembling in her hand. "I just wanted to come over and say hi."

I stand. "Bullshit. I haven't changed, Brooklyn. You have. I'm not going to let you wipe out the last three years like nothing happened just so you can feel good about yourself."

I head to Dylan on the playground, staying to the edge of the play structure and away from Brooklyn's friends. She stands up from the bench and goes to join the other girls. They don't glance my way when they leave the park and I return the favour.

"Jesus, Butch, you've got to be shitting me!" We are playing Spite and Malice, an old family-favourite card game. Butch has just played seven consecutive cards from his pile and four of them have been wild, meaning he can place them on any of the open stacks on our table.

"Jameson, watch your language! Honestly. Have some respect for your grandfather." Val pauses peeling carrots at the sink to sip her white wine. She turns her head to glare at me, but I don't look over, so it fails to land.

Tim is as exasperated as I am. "I thought you were supposed to be sick," he says.

"Not sick enough to lose to the likes of either of you." Butch is still playing, drawing another five cards for his hand to continue his reign of holy terror.

I lean back in my chair and glance down at my phone on my lap. Nothing from Cole, Lawrence, or even Brooklyn. She's probably waiting for me to apologize but she'll be waiting a long time. She owes me one instead.

"Is Dad coming home soon?" Tim asks. I can't bear the naked hope in his young voice. It's Sunday night and we haven't seen much of Ed this weekend. He says he has a big presentation at work this week to prep for, but I was reading at midnight last night and I heard their tightly controlled voices through our thin walls, arguing about money, my acting, Ed's long hours, Butch's health, and a host of other shit. I'm guessing his absence this weekend has more to do with Val than work, but Timmy doesn't know this.

Val is now slicing carrots on our apple-shaped wooden cutting board. "He knows dinner is at six. If he doesn't show up we'll eat without him and have fun on our own."

Tim's mouth is in a clamped line. He told me this morning that his stomach was hurting. I nudge his foot under the table and make a face at him to lighten the mood.

Butch sighs and discards to finally end his turn. He pulls himself to a standing position, still favouring his left leg where they did the biopsy on the growth. Val rushes forward, treating her father like he's a toddler. "Don't get up, Dad. You need to rest. I'll get you whatever you need."

"I need to stretch my back. Not sure you can help me with that." I snicker. Tim's pale face brightens a bit. I play two cards and then I have no other moves to make. Tim draws three cards and studies the stacks on the table like he's taking an exam.

"That roast beef smells terrific, hon. It's sure going to beat hospital food." Out of the corner of my eye, I watch as Val rubs Butch's arm. How can he not see how crabby and fucked up Val is? I don't understand how Butch can be so loving toward her when she's been awful to me since I got home from babysitting Dylan, making snide comments about selfishness and not putting others' needs first. Butch is the ultimate peacemaker, always trying to smooth over any situation, but he can't seem to divert from the tension brewing under the surface here.

"Kids, did you see this peach crisp your mom made for dessert? She's worked hard all day on this meal."

"My tummy hurts," Tim says quietly.

"I don't like peaches," I say at the same time.

Val dumps the carrots into the double boiler on the stove. "You better finish that game. Dinner will be ready in ten minutes and I'd like someone to set the table."

"I'm about to win so we'll be finished right away." Butch makes his way back to the table and sits down. He smiles at me while picking up his cards. I've got nothing to give him in return. I feel a cold sensation in the pit of my stomach, tingling like a warning of some imminent danger. I don't know how to fix this. I could make Val happier with me, but the price is too high to pay. Timmy chews on his ragged thumbnail and looks down at his lap.

Butch is playing his last few cards when Edward's key turns in the front door lock. Something clenched inside of me releases a bit because he's made it home for Val's dinner. I hear the thunk of Ed's leather laptop bag in the entryway, and then he slips off his shoes and walks in to join us.

"Nice of you to show up just in time for dinner." Val's voice is glacial. A look passes over Ed's face that I've never seen before. It's something close to despair.

Butch tosses his cards facedown onto the table. "Well, kids, obviously I'm about to win but I'll spare you the defeat. Let's set the table for your mom." He stands and steps closer to Edward. "Did you finish your presentation?"

"Just about. I'll put the final touches on it tomorrow. How's the leg?"

"Better all the time. Let me pour you some wine."

Tim and I clean up the cards. I'm so glad Butch is here to help us make it through this hideous dinner.

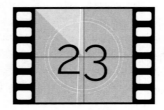

I stand alone on the curb in front of my school, a frozen fixture, while teens pour around me like rats from a sinking ship. Lawrence already walked past me on the way to the bus, but Cole offered to drive me because we are both going to work. Score! Yet another marvellous side benefit to having an older boyfriend—dare I say that? Even to myself? It might be too early, but even in my head the word sounds secure and hopeful. As a senior, Cole has a parking pass, but the lot is forever away so he said he'd drive up and get me at the curb.

I can hear his old silver Corolla before I can see it in the line of approaching vehicles. He's behind a Mercedes SUV and in front of a sleek BMW sports car. Cole paid for his Corolla himself and he's incredibly proud of it (a quality I find adorable). He pulls up and I open the rusty door and slide in beside him. Cole grins. "Hey buddy. Good to see you."

"It's not so bad looking at you, either." He drives off, shoulder checking for wandering kids, distracted parent drivers, and school buses. I take the opportunity to stare at his profile, soaking it up for when I need something pleasant to think of in the future.

"You ready for *Code Breakers* tomorrow? Butch still taking you?"

"Yes and yes. As ready as I'll ever be, I guess. I can't wait to get on set." I fiddle with my backpack strap. "Butch can chaperone. We'll have to take the bus and I have hair and makeup at eight in the morning. No test results yet, but at least his leg is better, so he can come."

"I wish I could drive you, but my classes are intense right now. Especially calculus and English. Mom is all over me about my grades and university applications. I can't miss any more school right now or she'll lose her fucking mind."

"It's totally fine. I get it. You're about to graduate."

"I'll be thinking about you all day. Text me updates. I think it's so cool that you're going to be working on this show. Mom is excited about it too."

I take a moment to allow this idea to spread through me. How amazing would it be to have a mom who was excited for me instead of pissed off? I try to focus on Cole thinking about me all day and Teresa being enthusiastic, so Val's crappy attitude doesn't pull me under.

Cole stops at a red light by the hospital. He glances at me and reaches for my hand. I curl my fingers into his, holding on. "What is it, buddy?"

I shake my head. "Val. And Ed. He worked all weekend, and when he came home for dinner she was cold and mean. Tim curled up into a ball at bedtime. He told me his stomach hurts, but Val made him go to school today. I heard my parents fighting late into the night on Saturday, about anything and everything. It feels like they are coming unglued."

The light turns green and Cole drives forward, but he squeezes my hand and strokes the base of my thumb with his. "That's really shitty, Jamesy. When my parents split, the fighting got bad for a long time and then it seemed better, but they still didn't make it. With your parents hopefully this is just a short-term thing. They didn't use to fight like this, did they?"

"No, they didn't. I wonder how much of it has to do with me and my acting." Admitting this hurts more than I thought it would. I feel panicky, like I'm supposed to choose between my parents loving each other and following my dreams. What if one thing hinges on the other?

Cole pulls his car into the Lantern parking lot. He turns off the ignition with his left hand, takes off his seatbelt, and swivels his body toward me. I don't know if I can make eye contact with him. My insides are like sandpaper. Is this too much for Cole to handle? Do I seem like a snivelling little girl to him?

Gently, he tilts my chin up with his free hand. My eyes are teary, but looking at his green eyes calms me, the way I feel settled when I stare at the ocean. "There's no way your acting has to do with your parents fighting. The two things are separate. I learned this when my mom made me go to therapy when I was thirteen, so I know what I'm talking about."

"But you're not an actor." It's a dumb attempt at humour, but Cole's mouth pulls up in a hint of a smile.

"True. But I know what I'm talking about."

I draw a long, wavering breath. I lean toward him, ever so slightly, just for the sheer reassurance of his solid presence. He covers the rest of the distance between us, touching his mouth to mine and running his hand through my hair. Val, Edward, Tim, Teresa—they all melt away, disappearing under the kiss as it builds, our breath steaming up the windows and keeping us warm.

INT. DEN - NIGHT

Jameson Harper as Beekdal kneels behind a large mahogany desk. The safe clicks and opens.

                    BEEKDAL
    And you said it couldn't be done.

Ken rushes forward, a knife glinting in the firelight. He plunges it into Beekdal's back.

                    FRANNY
    What the hell, Ken? We might still need her.

Beekdal turns around, shocked. She tries to come to her feet, leaning on the desk and moving toward Franny and Ken.

                    BEEKDAL
    I knew I couldn't trust you! I told you, Franny, he's a damn rat.

                              KEN
          Splitting this two ways instead of three
          is simply good fiscal sense.

Ken steps around Beekdal to the safe. He
starts pulling out wads of cash and jewels.

                            FRANNY
          I'm sorry, Beekdal. I've learned a lot
          from you.

Beekdal falls to the ground.

                            BEEKDAL
          Rot in hell, Franny.

As she dies, sirens wail outside, getting
closer. Ken and Franny exchange panicked
looks. Franny steps over Beekdal's body and
looks under the desk.

                            FRANNY
          That bitch pressed the panic button!

                            DIRECTOR
          Cut! Nice take. Let's reset and do it
          again.

                             →⦁←

    I walk through the soundstages to my trailer (my very own
trailer, with a masking tape "Beekdal" slapped haphazardly on
the door). A light rain is falling, so I'm using my purple happy-
face umbrella. The crew is setting up for the turnaround, which
will point the camera at me for my close up as I perish from my
fake knife wound. If I star in a feature film one day, I don't know

if I'll ever be as thrilled as this. I can't imagine anyone in their entire life having more fun and getting paid for it than me today.

I climb the three stairs to my trailer and open the metal latch on the door. Butch is so still on the sofa that my heart catches. I cough lightly and his eyes flutter open. "There's my duck!" He rolls to a sitting position. "How was the death scene?"

"Pretty damn fabulous. I might ask if I can keep the prop knife when the shoot is over." I sit down beside him on the velvety blue sofa. "Are you okay?"

"I'm great. Someone dragged me out of bed at five forty-five a.m., so I'll need a few little dozes today."

I reach for my phone. "I thought all seniors got up at the crack of dawn."

"Only the crazy ones." Butch stands and stretches, still favouring his sore leg. He walks to the small fridge and pours more cream into his coffee. Some candy and snacks lie scattered on the kitchen counter but he ignores these, even though the red licorice smell is seriously enticing.

My phone is lit with texts from Sam, Lawrence, Cole, and even Brooklyn.

> Happy shoot day to my #1 client! (don't tell the others) Can't wait to hear everything and I'm working on more auditions for you! ☺

> Hey movie star. Don't forget me when u big. You owe me for all the fucking improv Wu made us do. Steal me some decent food from crafty pls

> Poor Beekdal, getting killed today. You're too young and cute to die. I'm so not ready. Lantern will seem lame now to you but I'll be here waiting. See you soon buddy

> Jamesy, congrats on your first role. I'm really happy for you.

Brooklyn's text is baffling, but the other three make me smile. So what if there's nothing from Val or Edward? I have to stop expecting them to have a sudden change of heart. I'm here, on a real set, getting paid fifty-five bucks an hour on an actual union voucher for principal rate as an actor. With this credit, I can apply for apprentice status in the union. This is the big time. Butch is here, Cole is waiting for me, Lawrence is peppier and back to his usual self. (Focus on right now, Jamesy. No sad thoughts today. This is too fucking fabulous for that.)

A knock sounds on the metallic door and then I hear the P.A.'s voice. "Jamesy? They're ready for you."

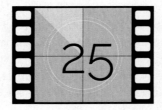

"Take one more deep breath, noticing how you feel at this exact moment, and then open your eyes." Mrs. Wu's voice has a hypnotic quality to it. I hate to open my eyes, but drama class is over and the bell is about to ring. I have science next, and likely another argument with Kuntz about missing school yesterday for *Code Breakers*. Sigh. Why can't drama just go all day?

I look around the circle. Lawrence appears to be asleep, and Brooklyn has a huge shit-eating grin on her face like she discovered the winning lottery ticket in her hand. Mrs. Wu waits until all eyes are open and people are stretching before saying, "Don't forget that I want every monologue memorized by next class." A bunch of people groan and she raises her voice over the grumbling. "No more excuses. Jamesy memorized her lines for the TV show yesterday in a matter of days. You've all had weeks. Get it done!"

The bell sounds, and I reluctantly come to my feet. I can see Brooklyn walking toward me so I frantically try to get Lawrence's attention, but he's grabbing his backpack and talking with Kelsey. I feel like a trapped animal. Suddenly she's in front of me.

"How did it go yesterday on set?"

"It was fun." I start walking to my stuff at the back table. Brooklyn tags along.

"I hope your call time wasn't insanely early. Once I had to leave my house by four a.m. to make it into North Vancouver. It was brutal."

I don't feel like any response is necessary, so I say nothing, even though I want to say, "At least your mom drives you everywhere and you don't have to take the bus." I grab my books and my backpack and turn to leave the classroom.

"Did you get my text yesterday?" Okay, now I'm irritated. (Way to make it always about you, Brooklyn.) What the hell is going on with her lately? She must have pissed off her new and improved friends.

I turn to face her. Science is just down the hall, so I can spare a minute or two. Lawrence is long gone, the jerk. "Yes, I got it. I was surprised you bothered."

Brooklyn blinks at me. She swallows and fidgets. "I don't know why we can't get past whatever is wrong between us. I miss you as a friend."

"I find that hard to believe. You decided to stop talking to me. I waited around for you to be decent toward me again for over a year and now I have better friends too, ones I can count on. What's wrong between us is you being a shitty friend and it's not something I can just get over."

"Well, we're both actors and we should be supporting each other, not competing."

This time I actually laugh. "Come on, Brooklyn, really? When you were booking roles, it was all about you. I bet you were hoping I'd never book anything. But now I have, and suddenly we should support each other? I didn't realize you were so funny."

I start walking out of the classroom, hoping she'll get the hint and move on. But no, because she's Brooklyn, she falls into step with me as we navigate the hallway traffic. She puts out a hand and touches me on the forearm. Her nails are a pale lilac with a white flower painted on the ring-finger nails. "Jamesy, it seems like you want me to apologize but this isn't all my fault. We grew apart. That happens to people. But now it would be lovely if we could grow back together."

I stop in the hallway, shrugging her hand away from me. "I'll tell you what would be lovely. To jump in a time machine and go back to when you were a decent person. We used to tell each other everything. Remember how fun our sleepovers used to be? And how we'd text each other stupid shit our parents used to say? And how we made twenty bucks that time on our lemonade stand and blew it at the corner store on so much candy that we puked the next morning? Then we got to grade eight and you saw a chance to dump me for more popular girls and you took it. Now you want me to forget that the last few years ever happened and just smile sweetly and carry on like nothing has changed. That's too much to ask, even for you. I've gone through a ton of stuff now without you, so I think we should just leave it at that."

This time when I walk away, she doesn't come after me. I feel a hollow sort of sadness in my belly, but I don't know what to do about it. I spent way too many nights crying over Brooklyn ignoring me to give in to her now that she's turning on the charm again. It's too risky. If she truly misses me as a friend, she can show her loyalty to me by doing something besides using fancy words.

My phone bleeps as I walk into science just before the bell. I slide into my desk, dropping my books and backpack on the floor by my feet, and glance at my phone before Ms. Kuntz makes us put them away.

Romance MOW audition tomorrow morning!! Sides emailed later today. You're on fire!

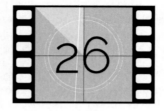

"Was it everything you hoped it would be?" Grace's face is lit up with a smile to rival the sun. I'm perched on the edge of her messy desk at the Lantern's back office.

"Yes. And then some. Butch had a nap in my trailer, just like you'd see in a movie about Hollywood. With my character's name on the door on a piece of masking tape! And I had my own production assistant who walked me to and from set and answered any questions I had. I didn't want it to end."

Grace leans forward to sip from her cold coffee. "Don't worry, Jamesy. You'll book something else. This is going to happen for you. I just know it."

"My agent Sam got me an audition for a romance MOW tomorrow at ten thirty. It's only a few lines but if I book it, I can get back on set. Now I need two more credits and I can apply for full membership in the actor's union, which means higher pay and medical benefits and a ton of cool stuff!"

"I'll cross every finger and every toe for you. But how's your mom about you missing school for these auditions?"

I stand up and stretch like a cat. "She doesn't exactly know. And I think we should keep it that way."

Grace makes the old-school gesture of zipping her fuchsia-lipsticked mouth and elaborately tosses the imaginary key. "Break a leg, my girl."

"Thanks. You're the best boss ever." I walk to the door and turn back to blow her an over-the-top kiss (to match her wild outfit of black leather pants, plunging V-neck sweater, floral scarf, and four-inch platform heels). "Better go see if Cole's made it in yet."

I walk out of Grace's office and enjoy the tickling warmth I feel spreading through me. Why is it my employer can cheer me on but my parents can't? Does it really cost Val that much to say, "Good luck," or "I'm proud of you," or even "It takes guts to go after your dream?" Apparently, the price is too high. I'll have to enjoy Grace's kindness and try my best to make it stretch to cover my parents, too.

Cole isn't in the lobby, but the first show isn't until four, so the main doors are still locked. I hear the clank of the metal dusting pan in cinema one. He must be sweeping in there. I step in and see him near the screen, just as he looks up and spots me. Cole's smile is slow and broad. He abandons the broom and the pan, leaning them against the front row of seats, and walks toward me.

"Hi," I say before his mouth covers mine. His lips taste salty and delicious. Both of his arms circle my waist. Oh God, his body is so hard. What if mine feels soft to him? I should work out more or stop trying to get out of P.E. class. (Focus, Jamesy, he's kissing you!) Cole hugs tightly, so there's no space between our bodies. The kiss goes long, drawn out with a rising urgency and excitement. When he pulls back, we are both breathing heavily, which makes us laugh.

"Good thing Grace didn't pop in," I note. Cole's arms are still around me, so our faces are two inches apart.

"She's a romantic. I don't think she'd mind at all." Cole leans forward for one last kiss, gentler this time, with his hands drawing lazy circles on my lower back. "I missed you yesterday."

"I can tell. I thought about you so much on set. I wish you could've seen it all with me."

Reluctantly, Cole steps back. I grin at him, feeling like I could lift up off the ground and fly. He says, "Next time."

"It's a deal." I move toward the broom and the dust pan, sweeping up a stray straw by one of the aisle seats. "We better open the lobby doors. People will be here soon."

"For this piece of shit movie? We'll end up on our own."

"Works for me." We both walk out of the theatre. Cole takes the broom and the pan from me and puts them in the small closet near the concession. He goes to unlock the front door and I lean against the glass counter.

"My dad called me today," Cole says.

"Oh yeah? It's been a while since you've talked to him, right?"

"He's been working in Calgary in construction. He said it's ridiculously busy and he can't hire enough people to help him this summer. He invited me to go out and work with him." I've been listening happily to Cole talk, but at the word "invited" I can sense that my lungs are freezing up. I hear a generalized ringing in my ears. My neck itches.

Cole comes back to me, his eyes bright. "Maybe this is the answer, Jamesy. I don't know what the hell to do about college. I just need some time to get myself sorted out. Getting a change of scenery seems like the right move. And my dad is laid-back compared to Mom, who wants me to conform to the standard pattern of university for four years and then some reliable fucking job in a suit and tie for the rest of my life."

Honestly, I didn't hear much of that speech. I must be breathing again, because I didn't pass out, but how can we go from making out in cinema one to him moving to Calgary next month in the span of three minutes? Cole seems thrilled with this idea of moving, but how in the bloody world do I fit into this harebrained plan? I realize with a start that Cole is waiting for me to say something.

"Wow, this is a big surprise." The words sound like gibberish to me. I force myself to ask the question, "How long do you think you would be gone?"

Cole moves around me to straighten up the stack of popcorn bags. He seems to need some activity to focus him. "I don't know. I guarantee that Mom will flip when I mention it to her, so I wanted to talk to you first. Kind of as a practice." He stops fiddling with the bags and looks at me.

I force my face to relax, in case it wears the pained expression that I'm definitely feeling inside. I regulate my breathing for a second, trying to choose my words carefully so I don't unintentionally sound like Val. "You seem excited about spending some time with your dad and trying the construction thing. I just wish it were here and not a province away."

Cole leans over the glass counter and takes both of my hands. "It's only an idea. I wouldn't want to be away from you, either. We'll just have to wait and see what happens." He smiles and squeezes both of my hands. The bell on the door tinkles softly, ushering in a group of seniors.

"Welcome to Lantern!" I say in a stellar imitation of a happy person.

When I come down the stairs into the kitchen before school, I see Val typing on her laptop at the table. Her whole body appears tense, like she's holding everything in and the strain is getting to her. Quietly, I pull a banana from our white ceramic two-decker fruit stand on the island and wonder if I can grab a cinnamon-apple cereal bar from the pantry without alerting Val.

"How was your acting thingy?" Tim inquires from the living room, his head bowed over his iPad as he sprawls on the couch in his underwear. I sigh. Val looks up, a frown darkening her face.

"It was terrific, Tim, thanks for asking. The best day of my life." Now that my cover's blown, I open the pantry and rummage around.

"I had an email from the school office about your attendance this month. They didn't say the word 'truancy,' but that's the next conversation I'm likely to have with them." Val's voice sounds like an elastic band stretched to its breaking point. "I don't understand you, Jameson. You're risking your entire future with this foolishness."

My heart races, revving up like a car engine. I can feel my face flushing. I see black spots in front of me and suddenly I'm afraid I'm going to fly off the handle and start screaming obscenities. Then this tentative truce really will be over for good. I glance to my right, anywhere but Val, and see Tim staring at me with wide eyes. He's still, like a statue, and his fear is palpable. I return to myself when Tubbs winds himself around my leg, purring and hoping to be picked up.

I wait until my breathing returns to normal, taking my time pulling my water bottle out of the fridge and putting it in my backpack. When I speak, my voice sounds low and barely audible. "I can't keep having the same fight with you. I refuse to do it."

I walk to the front door and offer Tim a tight smile. It's goddamn seven twenty in the morning, and she has to start in at me. If Tim hadn't looked at me with such terror, I may have finally told Val exactly what I think. Maybe I should find an alternate place to stay first, but bad things are ahead for me and Val. I can sense it. As I'm putting on my Keds, I hear Ed's light footsteps rushing down the stairs. He pours a travel mug of coffee and comes to join me at the door in a suit. I notice that he's carrying a small overnight bag.

"Any chance you can drive me into the city? I have an audition for a TV movie this morning."

Edward digs in the closet for his black leather lace-ups. "Sorry, James, can't do it. I'm going out of town for a few days for work."

Tim stands up and comes to Edward. His lower lip is trembling, like it used to when he was a toddler. "Why do you have a suitcase, Daddy?"

Reaching out a hand, Edward messes up Tim's red hair. "It's no big deal. I won't be gone too long. Mom will be here."

I look behind Edward to see Val, standing in her rose-pink robe with her arms crossed over her chest. It's like we are all wax figures. Nothing feels real. I rub my bare arms, as they have broken out in goosebumps.

Tim is properly crying now, fat silent tears that drip from his chin to the hardwood. "When are you coming back? Are you mad?" Tim walks around Edward to me, pressing his wiry body into my side. "Jamesy, what's going on?"

"I don't know, Timmy. And it doesn't look like our parents are too interested in telling us. I guess we're on our own. I'd stay with you, but I've got to take a bus to my audition as Edward is leaving and refuses to drive me, and then I have to go to school so I don't fuck up my future. Sorry."

I pull myself away from Tim, open the door and run down the stairs. As I speed walk to the bus stop, I picture Cole's face, hoping it will help me calm down. I run my lines for the MOW audition. I obsess over Brooklyn and her recent friendliness. I wonder what's going on with Lawrence and his hard-ass dad. Anything but Tim's haunted face, Ed's overnight bag, and those round wet splashes on the floor.

Thursday, May 9th

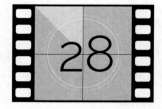

I'm in a depressing waiting room that reminds me of a cheap dentist (with a similarly unpleasant chemical smell), waiting to be called for my TV movie audition. Sam texted me a good luck message while I was standing on the bus with the other harried commuters. I tried to go over my lines, but I was too distracted by the Val and Edward show earlier. I hope Tim is okay at school. His face was desperate this morning, like someone drowning and grasping for a lifeline that is just out of reach.

My fingers are trembling, but I grab my phone to distract myself. Actors are coming and going from the audition room, while the tall, willowy, twenty-something woman who works for the casting director calls names from her clipboard. They are behind schedule, as usual, but I'm okay with sitting here in this drab space with its grungy coffee-coloured carpet and wrinkled movie posters covering plaster cracks on the off-white walls. I feel slightly panicky, like I'm sliding off the edge into something really frightening. I text Cole, hoping he'll see it and respond right away.

> A total shitshow at my house today. Ed might be moving out. Tim crying. Val an ice cold bitch as usual. Waiting to audition and I miss you so much. I think I might be falling for you, buddy

I hit send before I can chicken out. My insides are churning, but if one thing is clear to me, it's how I feel about Cole. I'm pretty sure I don't believe in God, but just in case I find myself whispering, "Please God, let him stay." A hipster guy with rolled-up jeans and a man-bun glances my way but then goes back to his script. We're all actors here, and mumbling out loud before an audition goes with the territory.

No dots. Cole must be in a class where he can't use his phone. Either that or I freaked him out and he's currently booking a flight to Calgary, but I can't think about that or I'll lose my mind. My phone buzzes, and I realize I've been holding my breath. I look down to see it's Lawrence.

> Hey bitch, Kuntz pissed your gone again. She might call Val. Thought I shd warn you!

I pinch my lips together. Goddamn Kuntz. (Get laid, woman, and leave me alone for once!) I'm thinking about what to text Lawrence when this bombshell comes through.

> Speaking of shit you shd know, there's a chance I'm crushing on Darren who lives on my street. We've been playing basketball and I think he's into me but I don't fucking know what this means. Are we still friends if I'm gay or is it all over

I text back furiously, a big grin on my face.

> Larry Boy, you beautiful bastard—you know I love you forever and always! If you're gay I'm thrilled but you liked that horrible Erin in grade 8 so maybe bi? We need to talk more about this! And I must get a peek at this dude and make sure he's good enough for you. xoxoxo

After a few seconds, I get a series of random emojis in response, which is Lawrence's way of saying he's relieved. I can't imagine his dad will react well to news of this Darren guy. Will Lawrence have to pretend they are just friends if their relationship progresses into something? Oh God, I hope not. It's not the Middle Ages.

For some reason, Butch pops into my head. I hope he's recovered from his leg thing and is back to normal now. That nap in my trailer (TRAILER!) the other day wasn't like him. It's taking forever for these biopsy results to come through. I pull up my texts with Butch and I'm just starting to type when I hear, "Jameson Harper?" I slide my phone into my pocket, smile at the statuesque casting assistant goddess, and follow her down a long hallway to one of the closed doors.

She knocks and then opens the door to reveal the usual folding table with three people behind it, a camera, and an area for me to stand and read. The assistant announces me to the team members, who have pleasant expressions on their faces. I have the bizarre sense that I'm not actually in this dreary room. I'm miles away from here, floating somewhere alone, untethered to anyone or anything.

"Okay, Jameson, whenever you're ready. Look into the camera and slate, then Peter will read with you."

I turn toward the camera, open my mouth, and I'm surprised when words tumble out.

Thursday, May 9th

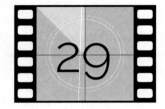

Scenery moves past the bus windows, softened by spring drizzle, and suddenly I decide that I can't face going back to school for my last two blocks. All I can see is Tim's scared face, Ed's suitcase by the front door, and Val's arms crossed over her chest. I know I shouldn't skip, because I've missed so much the last few weeks and Val is itching for a fight, but I don't feel strong enough to face Ms. Kuntz or anyone else. The only person I want is Cole, so badly that I put my arms around my shoulders to give myself a hug. He's at school, so I decide on the next best thing. I pull the cord to stop the bus.

I dial my phone as I walk. It's picked up on the second ring. "Hello? Jamesy?"

My heart's in my throat, trying to escape my body. "Teresa? I know Cole's at school, but I wondered if you were home."

"Yeah, I'm here."

"Any chance I can stop by?"

"Sure, but aren't you supposed to be in class?"

I'm in front of the burgundy door now. My voice feels like it's tied off in a tourniquet. I speak, but it comes out garbled and mushy. "I'm outside."

I hear movement in the house, then the door swings open to reveal Teresa in black yoga pants, a mint-green zip-up sweatshirt, and her hair in a high ponytail. She has no makeup on and she looks young. Her brow furrows as she takes me in. My face crumples like a paper bag, my eyes overflowing with hot tears. She opens her arms and I step into them, hanging on like a little kid.

→ ←

I sip my virgin pina colada, the sugar giving me a boost of much-needed energy. After I cried for what seemed like an hour, Teresa suggested I clean up a bit and that we go out for lunch. My face is still puffy and my eyes look like I'm coming off a bender, but sitting on the patio at Marvin's Bistro among normal people going about their Thursday is helping me calm down. We just shared a spinach dip appy and we're waiting for our meals to arrive (club sandwich for her and quesadillas for me).

"I'm so glad you came to me," Teresa says. "You can't keep this stuff bottled up. Is Cole not willing to talk with you about it?"

"No, he is, but Ed's never packed a suitcase before and left. He says he's on a business trip but I don't buy it. That was just this morning, and Cole's busy right now with finals and grad."

She nods. "I know you said it's hard to talk to your parents about how you feel, but I think you should try. They have to know how much this is affecting you."

"It's useless. It doesn't help at all." I sound mutinous, like a toddler with a pouty lip.

"I remember how awful it was, going through my divorce. I was so focused on myself that I found it hard to notice what was happening with Cole. If I could go back and do it differently, I would." Teresa runs her fingers down her water glass, making lines in the condensation. "Your parents are hurting right now. Give them some time to sort it all out and know that whatever they are fighting about is separate from you and your brother. Keep talking to me, and to Cole, and to your grandfather and any other friends who make good listeners. We're here." She smiles.

"I don't think Val and Ed would be fighting if I weren't pursuing acting. Maybe if I give it up, everything will go back to the way it was before." Oh God, the tears are coming back, rising like vomit in my throat. I swallow them down, drawing breaths in short gulps, trying not to lose it here on this cheery patio.

Teresa leans forward and puts her hand over my icy-cold one. "No way. It's not your fault. If you quit acting, they would find something else to fight over. That's not the answer, Jamesy, believe me."

Our server comes over with our plates, setting them in front of us. "Is there anything else I can get you right now?"

"No, I think we're okay," Teresa says.

The server walks away. I play with a yam fry, but I don't know if I can eat. I want everything to be okay. I don't want to give up acting. I want Cole to stay with me. I wish Teresa was my mom instead of Val.

I lift up a wedge of my quesadilla, the melted mozzarella forming an umbilical cord back to the next piece. "Thanks for bringing me here," I say. "This looks delicious."

Thursday, May 9th

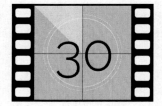

Even on my bed upstairs with my headphones blaring the *Mean Girls* Broadway soundtrack, I can still hear a knock at our front door. Because the door is metal, it makes an echoey sound that I tend to feel in my body. I turn the volume down on my phone and glance at my alarm clock. Nine-thirty p.m. I hold my breath, hoping it's Edward, but would he really knock at his own door?

I'm attempting to catch up on homework, but I'm not getting far. Cole hasn't answered my text from earlier this morning at the audition. My face goes hot when I think about saying, "I'm falling for you." We've only been together a couple of weeks and nothing's been defined. I can sense an ice cube forming in my digestive system when I think about him looking at that text and choosing not to respond. Somehow this image is worse than everything else that's going on.

The door opens with a rush of air, followed by Val's voice. "Can I help you?"

"I'm looking for Jamesy." At Cole's voice, my torso turns to cooked spaghetti. The relief is in my hands, my legs, my insides. He's here. I didn't scare him away. Scrambling off my bed, knocking textbooks and binders and lounging cats to the floor, I rush past Tim's bedroom, where he's sleeping, and race down the stairs, skidding to a stop by Val.

Cole stands under the harsh entryway light. His face softens when he sees me, and he pulls out his phone from the pocket at the back of his jeans. He holds it up. The screen is smashed in a thousand points of glass, an intricate spiderweb of destruction. "This happened in the parking lot first thing. Riley grabbed for it and next thing I know, it's face-down on the ground. Toast."

"That sucks bad." (He wasn't ignoring my text!!!) We're conversing as if Val isn't standing here, but then she clears her throat and I make a snap decision. "Wanna go for a walk?" I ask Cole. "Get some air?"

He nods. I step forward to shove my feet into my Keds and I grab a hoodie from the hooks by the door. "Jameson, it's quite late and you have homework to do."

"I won't be long." I take a key from a hook and nudge Cole quickly out the door. We hurry down the steps and I pull him away from our townhouse. I can imagine Val standing by the glass doors leading out to the deck, straining to see what we might be up to.

"Slow down," Cole says. I drag him until we turn the corner of our building and I know we are away from Val's line of sight, then I push myself into him, breathing in his cinnamon aftershave smell. He tucks his phone away and strokes my hair with his hand. "I was out with Riley and Big Dave, but when I got home Mom said you were upset, so I came right over. Val didn't look too happy to see me, but I'm glad you are."

I tip my face up to him and he moves his hand around to my cheek. I come up onto my toes and press my mouth to his, using my tongue to inch inside. I long to possess him, to really feel him, to lose myself completely in who he is.

A tween boy walks by with his dog on a leash. "Get a room," he grunts under his breath. Cole and I break apart and he laughs.

"Come on," I say. "I have an idea." We walk to the clubhouse near the front gate of our complex. I use the fob on my key ring to get us inside and onto the pool deck. The pool won't open for another couple of weeks, but it's deserted and there are a few lounge chairs scattered around. Cole pulls two together and flops down into one. I ignore the second chair and straddle Cole on his. He's surprised, but his arms come around me. I lean closer, kissing his neck.

"Hey. Jamesy. What happened today?"

I continue kissing him, yanking his shirt up so my mouth can reach more of him. His chest is strong and hard and I experience a fresh new level of arousal. I can feel his body stirring beneath me. My hands roam, like they have a mind of their own. I want to go farther than I've gone before. Cole's fingers find my breast and he squeezes gently, driving me wild. I cover his mouth with mine, and our kiss is wet and insistent. I'm grinding on him, when he inches away.

"No, don't stop," I breathe. "I want you." His hand drops from my chest and he pushes me to the side of the chair. I'm now on my side, with my head tucked near his chin.

When he speaks, his voice is cloudy. "I want you too, Jamesy, so goddamn much it's killing me to stop. But Mom said you were crying on our doorstep today, texting me and I couldn't answer because I broke my phone, and I want to make sure you are okay."

I start crying, in the inky darkness, and Cole shifts his position to pull me close. We stay like that for a while, until I'm strong enough to talk to him, to tell him how lost and scared I feel but that everything is more manageable now that I know I didn't frighten him away.

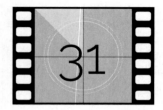

I type a text to Edward as I walk to the smoke pit at lunch. The sun is shining, and it's the kind of spring day that poets go on about. A light breeze, the smell of lilacs in the air, now compromised by cigarette and weed smoke as I approach forty or so students in a badly organized circle at the edge of school property. I continue to type with one thumb while periodically scanning the crowd for Lawrence and trying not to trip on the uneven grass and pavement.

> Tim is really upset abt you being gone. Can you call him at least? Anything I can do to make this better so you can come home? Where are you, anyway? Text me back!

I'm pissed that Edward has gone silent on me. He does this when he's under stress, but to disappear and leave us alone with Val in a murderous rage? (Fucking A solid parenting move, Ed.) I see Lawrence standing with a group of kids I don't recognize. One has a jet-black mohawk and the girl next to him has a face full of piercings (going through airport security must be a real bitch for her). Lawrence is puffing on a cigarette, holding it like a '40s movie star.

"Hey. You smoke now?" He sputters, taking another long pull to disguise this.

"Yeah, I'm giving it a whirl. Thought I'd add to the confusion and see if it helps clarify anything." He passes me the cigarette and I take it from him, rolling it around in my fingers and enjoying tapping the ash on the gravel under my feet. The metal-faced girl sneers at me, so I tug on Lawrence's oversized striped dress shirt with patches on the elbows and hiss at him to come talk to me.

He takes the smoke from my fingers and offers a small wave to his new group. When we are a few feet away and closer to the trees, I whisper, "Who are these people? That girl looks like she wants to slit my throat."

Lawrence shrugs. "Maybe. Being a little scared makes you feel alive."

I laugh, because he's so ridiculous and because he's mine. I thread my arm through his and lean against him while serial killer girl frowns. "She's probably in love with you. Poor thing. Speaking of love, tell me more about Darren. I want to meet him. Oh, and I texted Cole that I might be falling for him, but his phone is smashed and he never got it. Do I take it back or double down and tell him in person?"

He takes a final drag on the cigarette and stomps on the butt, blowing smoke in my face. "Darren is out of this fucking world. You'll be in love too when you meet him and forget about this bougie movie-theatre Cole. And Darren plays the guitar so that's sexy as all hell." Lawrence disentangles his arm and turns to give me a bear hug. "It's finally happening for us, Jameson Harper. We are out there crushing hard." He pulls back and looks at me, his brown eyes wide. "Are you surprised I might be bi? Or gay? Or something other than boring and normal and straight as an arrow?"

"You've never been boring in your life. Or normal. But that's a good thing." The bell drills out over the field. We turn to walk back toward the school, slow enough to stay behind the other smokers. "What are you going to do about your dad?"

"Tell him absolutely nothing except what he wants to hear. Like always."

We're both quiet for a moment. Then I say, "If your dad finds out and it's nasty around your house, we should emancipate and get our own place. I'd have to bring Tim and the cats, and you'd have to bring Puddles, but think of the fun we could have."

"No way Val and Ed are staying split up. This is just a blip. Anyway, I'm waiting until you're super rich like my '80s movie-star heroes and then you can pay for everything. But I'll bring Darren too."

"Deal." I hope he's right about my parents. I also hope his dad doesn't ever know he's interested in dating a dude. And he didn't answer me about Cole and the "falling for you" unread text but after last night at the pool deck, I'm leaning toward telling him. Maybe he'll stay if he hears that from me. Or maybe he'll run for the hills…well, the Rocky Mountains of Calgary. (Maybe he'll say it back.)

We're almost to the back door of the school when I see Ms. Kuntz, heading straight for me like a missile. "I'm glad to see you at school, Jameson. I've emailed your mother about your science grade. It's dropping and you won't remain on the honour roll at this rate. You've got to take your school attendance more seriously."

(Goddamn you, Kuntz. I'm stressed up to here. How about a shred of compassion?) "I've got to get to P.E., Ms. Kuntz. I'll see you in science."

We walk past her into the school, and when the door closes behind us Lawrence turns his head to look over his shoulder back toward Ms. Kuntz and says loudly, "And I'll see you in hell."

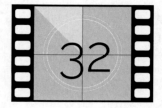

"Six of spades." The caller today for card bingo is a middle-aged man, the son of one of the residents. He has a porn-star mustache but speaks clearly when he draws a card and calls it out, which is a big improvement on the usual female caller, who mumbles. Half of the people playing have to crank their hearing aids up until they whine just to keep pace with the game. Now he repeats himself, drawing out each syllable so it feels like slow motion. "Siiiiiix of spaaaaaades."

Butch winks at me, but I can't summon the energy to acknowledge it. He knows something is wrong, but I came straight to Sunny Acres after school and we jumped right into card bingo, so there wasn't time to talk. This is our last hand, so as soon as someone bingos, the jig will be up about Val and Ed. Telling Butch is like acknowledging that their possible separation is real. I'm dreading it as much as the actual event of Ed moving out. I finish my lukewarm blueberry tea and avoid Butch's eyes.

"Queen of hearts." I have it in front of me and toss it in the centre as a woman behind me yells out, "Bingo!" Some residents sigh, others clap, a few grumble about how they only needed one more card called. The loonie for the winning hand is delivered by the caller and we tidy up the cards, saying, "Good game," to the other two competitors at our table.

"Got time before your beach party tonight to come talk to me?" Butch asks. I nod, and we head down the hall to his room.

"I didn't see Conrad at bingo today," I say to Butch. He stops, right before his door, and looks at me with a gentle expression. My eyes go wide.

"I'm so sorry to tell you, Ducky, but Conrad passed away. He had a stroke." I grab at Butch's sweater. It's all too much. Too sad. And the damn doctors told Val that Butch's biopsy results from the growth on his leg were "inconclusive," so we are stuck in this limbo of not knowing if he has cancer or he's fine. I can't lose him. I can't.

Butch opens his door, and once we are inside, I start to cry (yet again). Butch folds me in his arms, the best place in the world to be (other than Cole's arms now), and I use the front of his grey V-necked sweater as a handkerchief. He leads me over to his faded brown leather recliner, and settles me in it like I'm a colicky baby. Butch sits on the edge of the bed. I notice that he's still favouring the leg that had the biopsy.

He waits for me to be ready, watching me with a half-smile on his face. I love this about Butch. He doesn't rush you. After a long, wavering breath, I say, "Val and Edward are splitting up." I study Butch's expression, looking for shock and awe, but instead I find a sort of guarded resignation. "Ed packed a suitcase yesterday and said he was going away for a while. Now he's not answering my texts. Tim's a mess. Val's like a demon out for blood which isn't helping."

"Ducky, they're going to work this out."

"I don't know, Butch. It's been getting worse for a while now. Me booking acting jobs seems to be the final straw." I wipe at my nose with my sleeve. Butch gets up to grab me a box of tissues.

"No, it's not you. No way. I've been worried about them for the last year or more. But your mom and I are talking about it. Their marriage can be fixed, but it's not up to you to fix it. Just take care of yourself right now, and cut both of your parents some slack. Be patient with Timmy. You know how he worries."

"Can Tim and I come and stay here with you? I don't want to be at home right now. It's too awful there."

Butch looks around his tiny box of a room. "There's nowhere for you to stay, my love."

"We'll sleep on the floor! We don't need much space. Just a place where it's not so cold and scary for a little while. Please, Butch. Please."

I stand up and come to sit beside him on the bed. I lay my head against his shoulder. He smells like Irish Spring soap and coffee. His arm comes up and around me.

"You and Tim are both needed at home. Your dad will come to his senses and your mom will ease up on everything. She'll have to. I'll talk to both of them and fix this for you and for Tim. It's going to be okay."

He reaches across his body to hold my hand. I'm not sure of anything anymore but I do know that Butch loves me and will do his best to make things better. I have zero confidence in Val, but if anyone can help here, it's Butch. We sit like this for a while, until my tears dry up and I'm able to breathe without hiccupping.

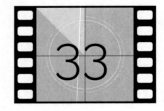

The bonfire crackles and spits as one of Cole's friends banks it up with more logs. Someone else pokes it with a hot dog stick, and a shower of sparks falls near my feet. Cole pulls me close, shielding my body with his while everyone laughs. I burrow into his torso, longing to stay like this forever. This night on White Rock beach. These marshmallows, dusted with sand. My third beer, helping me to relax and forget anything that doesn't belong here, with Cole and his grade twelve friends.

Perhaps he's thinking the same thing, because he leans down to kiss me. His face is blurry in the firelight. I lean over to lace my fingers with his. Big Dave, sitting next to Cole in our circle around the fire, hands Cole a joint. He puts it to his mouth and takes a drag, then passes it across me to the next girl, but I reach out to intercept it. I've never smoked weed but I've also never had three beers in one night. I clamp the blunt in my lips and inhale sharply, feeling cool as hell, and then promptly sputter and choke. Big Dave laughs. "Build up to it," he advises.

Cole takes it from me and hands it along. He squeezes my hand. "Want to go for a walk?"

I'm embarrassed by the tears in my eyes. I blink them away, then drain the rest of my beer. "Okay. I'll jush get another drink."

He stands and pulls me to my feet. "Later. I want to show you something."

We move away from the group at the fire. Cole supports me with his arm around my waist as I slowly realize I'm drunk. It's freeing to let go for once. I see Lawrence coming toward us, holding hands with a built guy I've never seen before. "Where are you two heading?" Lawrence asks. "We were coming to find you."

"Is this Darren?" I blurt out. "He's cute!"

They exchange glances and smile. "I can see you're letting loose tonight, James. Darren, meet Jamesy Harper and her boyfriend Cole. Yes, this is Darren, and yes, he's damn cute."

"Fucking A," I answer. "You better be nice to Larry Boy cause he's the bessht."

Cole starts moving again, taking me with him. He says, "See you guys in a bit." Lawrence and Darren walk toward the fire, waving back at me.

"Where we going?" I ask.

"There's this place under the path over here that I used to hide in as a kid. I hope it's still here. I want to show it to you."

In a few more steps, Cole slows down. I feel slightly dizzy and I'm happy to stop. He sits me down on a log and starts digging on his hands and knees. "This is it! When I was around ten I could fit my whole body in here."

I drop to my knees and crawl over to him. Cole fumbles with the flashlight on his phone to show me the small earthy space behind the logs and under the footpath. "Cool!" I crawl in as far as I can, not giving a damn about the damp sand on my jeans, and pull Cole in beside me. Our feet are sticking out, so we can't quite fit, but it's like our own private fort. I can still hear the waves lapping along the shore, but the sound is muted from here.

"I love it," I say, rubbing my hands along the sides of his face, then pulling him to me for a long kiss. His hands move down my back until he's cupping my butt. "Cole," I whisper between kisses. "I love you."

He pulls back to look at me in the darkness. Cole brushes the hair out of my eyes. He smiles. "I love you, too."

"Tell me you're not going to leave me. I don't want you to leave me, Cole. I need you." Tears are threatening to spill out and my words are jumbled and messy, but urgent. I clutch at him. "I want you. I love you. Have sex with me." I pull at his shorts, fumbling with his zipper, desperate for this moment not to slip away from me. He puts his hand over mine, pushing it away.

"We have time, Jamesy. Not like this, not when you've been drinking."

"We have no time! You could be leaving and I'm going to lose you. I want this, Cole, you aren't pushing it on me. I want you!"

He twists his body away, hiding the bulge in his pants, and kisses me again. "I can't imagine leaving you. That's the problem. I want this, too, but not tonight, with my friends just down the beach."

I realize suddenly that I still feel quite woozy. Cole crawls out of the hiding spot and then pulls me out after him. We lean against a log. "Did you really say you love me?" I ask.

"I really did. And you said it first. But I have another question for you."

I turn my head to look at his green eyes, fringed by dark lashes. God, I'm as horny as can be. I want to kiss him forever and get to the next part. He asks, "Will you go to grad with me?"

I grin, watery and drunk, and nod like he just proposed. He kisses me again, until I just can't stand the building pressure and my hands go roaming all over again.

Saturday, May 11th

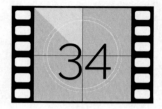

Slowly, I bring a bite of strawberry French toast to my lips. My hand shakes, but Val is distracted by her performance as a happy mother out for brunch with her adoring family, so she hasn't remarked on my obvious hangover. I'm on my fourth cup of coffee, which Butch keeps frowning at, but it's the only thing keeping the woodpecker in my brain subdued.

"Do you want another chocolate milk?" Butch asks Tim. He's barely made a dent in his scrambled eggs, sausage, hash browns, and toast. Tim slides them around with his fork, not making eye contact with any of us.

"Tim," Val calls. "Your grandfather asked you a question."

He mumbles, "I'm okay."

Butch reaches over and pats Tim on the arm. "Take your time, Red. No rush."

I finish my meal and try not to worry about Tim. Every few minutes a sense of warm joy washes over me, like the tide crashing into the shore, when I think about Cole saying, "I love you" last night. His face fills my imagination, cocooning us together in that special childhood place of his on the beach, where no one else can get in and ruin it. With every breath I just hear "Cole," again and again in a loop, remembering his mouth on mine and his hands touching me. None of this weird family stuff feels real compared to that.

"Jameson. Did you hear me?"

Cole's gorgeous face fades away, replaced by Val's insistent voice. She waves a hand in front of me. "Hello? Are you there?"

I push my plate away and reach for my cup of coffee, reluctantly turning toward her. "What is it?"

"I was telling both of you that your father is coming home for dinner on Sunday. I know you want to see him. Jamesy, I'd like you to be there."

"So Ed has officially moved out, then?"

"Of course not!" cries Val at the same time as Butch says, "Come on, Ducky." They exchange glances and Butch smiles at Tim like nothing at all is wrong. Val continues, "Your dad had to go away for a few days for work. No big deal."

(Yeah. Edward does all of his work travel on the goddamn weekends.) "Val, I'm not a little kid anymore. I'm sixteen years old. I'm a working actor in a TV show, with a string of auditions lined up. I have a boyfriend." (There's that liquid contentment flooding through me again!) "I'd like to be told what's really going on."

"And I'm telling you. Your dad will be coming for dinner tomorrow, and I'd like us all to eat together as a family." Val smiles, but it has an edge of menace to it.

Butch signals for the bill. He winks at me. I wonder when anyone gets permission from their family to grow up. I feel like I'd have to be at least forty before my parents and Butch saw me as anything other than a skipping kindergartener. What else do I have to do to prove I should be treated like an adult instead of patted on the head and told lies from morning to night?

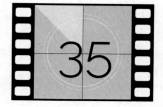

I reach for an "A," which slips from my hand, drifting in the light breeze down to the pavement. I'm ten steps up on a ladder in front of Lantern, changing out the weekly board for the movies. It should've been done yesterday, but Cole and I didn't work Friday, and obviously the new kid working decided to leave it for me. I've suggested a digital sign, but Grace says this manual board was good enough for decades and she doesn't see any reason to change it now, so here I am on a ladder.

I'm on my way down the ladder to retrieve the errant letter when I hear, "Don't come down. I'll hand it to you."

It's Brooklyn. She's alone, holding a half-eaten pretzel from the mall food court across the street. She bends down and picks up the "A," straining on her tiptoes to hand it up to me.

"Thanks." I slide it into place and add the final two letters to complete the board. I lower the plastic cover, then tuck the box of letters under my arm and carefully climb down the ladder.

"*Death by Pain*?" Brooklyn asks, reading the sign.

"All the decent movie titles have already been taken," I explain, shielding my eyes from the sun. "What are you doing here?"

"I was bored and wanted to get out of the house." She holds out the pretzel. "Want some?"

I shake my head. "I had a huge brunch at Marvin's earlier."

We stand for a few seconds, neither of us sure what the next move should be. Is she stalking me? Is that why she seems to run into me everywhere lately? "Well, I should get back inside. Good luck with the boredom." I start to walk toward Lantern's door.

"Jamesy, wait. Please." I turn back and wait. Brooklyn fidgets. She's always hated any form of confrontation, but I'm determined to make her talk first.

She gestures to a small wrought-iron bench. We both sit down. Finally, after what seems like the longest silence in recorded history, Brooklyn starts talking. "The summer between elementary and high school I worried a ton about not fitting in. I felt so babyish, so I changed my name and gave myself a whole new look for grade eight. You've always seemed so sure of yourself, but I've never felt like that. So when I met those girls at the barbeque on the first day, I thought they would help me find my way at such a big school. I kind of jumped ship over to them and I'm sorry. I thought you'd come too but you didn't seem to like them."

"I still don't like them. Do you?"

She shrugs. "I don't know. We don't have as much fun as you and I used to have. They don't like it when I talk about acting. It's all makeup and clothes and boys. I like feeling more popular, but I really do miss you."

"Okay."

"That's it? Okay?" Brooklyn turns toward me, wafting a flowery perfume in my direction. "Are we friends again?"

I laugh. "I don't know, Brooklyn-formerly-known-as-Balreet. Let's just see how it goes."

She smiles. "A truce?"

"Something like that."

"I'll take it." She takes a bite of her pretzel and I reach over to grab a chunk. It tastes sweet and doughy and salty. It reminds me of happier times.

I stand up. "I've got to get back to work. Cole's in there wondering why it's taking me so long to change out the sign."

"He's delicious. I'm mad jealous you landed him."

I shrug like it's nothing. "He's alright."

Brooklyn shoves me lightly in the shoulder. "Dating an older man. I'm sure your parents are thrilled with you."

"He's invited me to grad, but I don't think Val and Ed need to know about that. No sense burdening them with too much information."

"Definitely the right call. Let me know if you want help shopping for a dress."

The glass door of the Lantern swings open to reveal Cole in jeans and his purple golf shirt to match mine. "Hey. You coming back to keep me company?"

"Thinking about it. This is Brooklyn, by the way."

Cole steps outside to help me fold down the ladder. "Nice to meet you officially," Brooklyn says.

He reaches out his hand to shake hers. I hold open the door for Cole to walk past me with the ladder. Brooklyn makes a circle with her thumb and finger, then pokes her other index finger in and out of the hole, raising her eyebrows in sync with her finger jabs. I stick my tongue out and give her a goofy windshield wiper goodbye wave, like I used to do when we were little, and she laughs as she walks away.

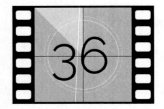

"Be careful with that wineglass, Jameson, it's slipping around in your hand. We got those as a wedding present."

I make a big show of setting it carefully on the table, then straighten a plate like I'm Carson in *Downton Abbey*. Val seems tense and on edge for this dinner with Edward. She made Tim wear clothes like we are expecting a formal guest instead of our dad, and she's been short with me all day (even though I've studiously avoided her).

"Who gave you the glasses?"

"Edward's old Aunt Maureen. She died when you were a baby, but I think they're crystal so they were probably expensive."

Val stirs the gravy on the stove, glancing every so often at the clock. She's dressed up, in a flowy emerald green skirt I've never seen and a sleeveless black top.

The knock at the door reverberates around our kitchen. It's strange for Dad not to walk in for dinner. Val looks at me, and in an instant, I register how weird she must be feeling about all of this. I start to walk toward the door, but Tim thunders up the stairs from the TV room and beats me to it.

"Daddy!" Tim flings himself at Edward like he's coming home from the war. I swallow hard. Ed smiles, trying to hurry inside before Tubbs darts outside. He hands me a large bunch of purple tulips and a bottle of white wine.

"Red, I swear you've grown in just a matter of days. And James, you're lovely as always." I lean in to kiss him on the cheek and I wait while he squeezes my arm. He takes off his dress shoes (dress shoes?!) and follows us into the kitchen.

Val sets the gravy boat on the table and turns to face us. "Hi.

Perfect timing." She gestures at the table. They both sound like they're delivering lines from a play, but at least they're talking. I set the flowers and the wine on the island, and we all sit down.

As we consume the roast chicken, coleslaw, lemon potatoes, and green beans with almonds, Tim beams around the table like everything is back to normal. Conversation is too stilted to feel comfortable, but I try to entertain them by embellishing my Brooklyn reunion and babbling on about the beach party on Friday night (obviously without mentioning getting drunk, smoking weed, or attempting to lose my virginity in a hollowed-out log). Both Val and Edward seem content to let me carry the dinner, so I decide to strike while the timing feels right.

"I've had a great week for acting, with a callback booked tomorrow for a role in a romantic TV movie, plus a commercial audition. If I get the commercial, it pays five thousand bucks, which would boost my college account, meaning less money that you'll both have to pay." I offer them my brightest smile, silently willing them to say something kind to me. (Please, please, please be proud of these accomplishments. Don't bark at me about school or wasting my life.)

Edward extends his fist across the table at me for a bump. He turns to Val, taking her temperature. She pastes a small smile on her face but doesn't say anything. Ed says, "I'm proud of you, James. You're a go-getter and this quality is going to serve you very well in life."

"Thank you. That means a lot to me." I toy with my remaining green beans and decide to press ahead, in case Val is tempted to ruin this warm and fuzzy moment for me. "It can be rough missing some school, but I do all of my work so I don't fall behind. If I didn't have to bus and Skytrain around it would make my life much easier, but it's worth it in the end because now I'm starting to book roles, so I don't want to lose this momentum."

"What time do you need to be in the city tomorrow?" Ed asks.

"Ten, so thankfully the bus won't be super early, but it will still take an hour and a half to get there."

"I'll drive you." I just about fall off my chair. My face must look stunned, because Edward laughs. "Really, I will."

"Where are you staying?" asks Val. Edward turns toward her and they seem to hold eye contact for a long moment, but this could be wishful thinking on my part.

"In Burnaby, at my brother's."

Next to me, Tim seems to be gearing up to speak but I reach over and squeeze his knee to get him to shut up. I can tell he was going to say something stupid about Edward being on a business trip and staying at a hotel. Val starts to stack plates. She stands up and walks toward the sink.

"No sense driving back to the city tonight if you are heading that way in the morning. It makes more sense to stay here."

"If you don't mind, that would be great." He pulls the potato dish toward him and gestures for us to help him clean up. Timmy and I grin at each other when Edward's back is turned.

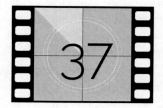

After circling Action Casting three times looking for parking in Mount Unpleasant (it's actually Mount Pleasant, an area near downtown Vancouver where many of the casting offices are located, but because it's crowded and bus service is challenging here, I've given it my own nickname), Edward finally finds a pay lot with an available spot. While he pays for parking, I engage in deep breathing to keep myself loose and calm for my commercial audition.

This morning I came downstairs early for some water and I found Ed sleeping on the couch. It seemed so out of place and sad. I made sure Tim didn't go downstairs until all evidence of Edward's sleeping spot was cleaned up. Better to let him think Val and Edward were in their bedroom as usual, at least for a little while.

My phone buzzes and I glance down to read as Edward joins me to walk the two blocks to the Action building.

> You're going to kill it today, buddy. Audition AND a callback. I'll think about you in fucking calculus. Can't wait to see you soon and pick up where we left off

"Who's that?" Ed asks.

"Cole. Wishing me luck for today."

"When am I going to meet this guy? I'd like to know who he is, and try to calm your mom down about him being so much older."

We arrive at Action Casting and I open the glass door. "He's a little more than a year older, which is nothing."

"Not at this age, James. When I was seventeen, I was only thinking about one thing."

"Ice cream?" I ask. He laughs. We climb the stairs to the second floor and head down the hall to Action's big brown door.

"Boy, you really know where you're going."

"Yeah. It's like I've taken the bus all the way here dozens of times on my own when every other kid has a parent with them." I can sense Edward looking sharply at me but I'm signing in and getting my photo taken against the white wall and then filling out my paperwork, so he has to wait. The room is crowded, as usual, with lots of teens and parents. I write my measurements, agent contact info and available dates on autopilot, aware of Edward taking in this scene for the first time.

When I finish the two pages and hand them to the assistant, I return to squeeze in on the bench next to Ed. "Thank you for driving me today. I appreciate it. But I really need something else from you." He turns his head. "I don't ask for much. But this is important, to keep Val off my back for a while. I need you to email my science teacher, Ms. Kuntz, and tell her that you give your permission for me to miss some school for acting. My grades are good and every other teacher is fine with my auditions, just not her. Please, Dad. I need your support and help here."

He takes a deep breath, clearly weighing multiple sides of this situation. "I'll think about it, Skittles. That's the best I can do."

"I'll take it. Thanks." I give him a small smile. My phone vibrates and we both look down. It's a picture of Lawrence and Darren, eating each other's faces off.

You're not the only skank gettin' some!

Edward raises his eyebrows (clearly, he has questions!), but thankfully my name is called. I stand, tuck my phone into my jeans, and hurry into the audition room.

INT. CASTING OFFICE — DAY

The CASTING DIRECTOR (45) addresses JAMESY and the other THREE TEENAGE GIRLS who have entered the room.

CASTING DIRECTOR
Good morning. This spot is for Neutrogena,
so we need you to pretend to wash your
face while looking into the mirror. Then
your line is "Ready for school, for a
date, for sleep, and for hanging out!"

One by one, the girls slate and go down
the line following this instruction by
enthusiastically repeating this peppy tag
line.

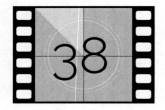

INT. CASTING OFFICE — DAY

JAMESY HARPER as ROSE BROWNING (16) looks
beyond the camera to her MALE READER (28),
an earnest expression on her face.

                    ROSE
    I'm so relieved you said that. I was
    hoping you felt the same way, but I
    didn't want to assume…
            (she barks out a laugh)
    Okay, I'll stop THAT now and get back
    to normal.

Rose raises her eyebrows at the reader.

                 CASTING DIRECTOR
    I liked that adlib at the end. You've got
    an interesting take on the character.

The DIRECTOR (47) nods.

                    DIRECTOR
    You have a quality we're looking for.

(beat)
Thanks for coming in. We'll be in touch.

JAMESY

Thank you!

→ ←

I stroll into the waiting room, humming a show tune from *Come From Away* under my breath, and snap my head back in surprise at the sight of Edward scrolling through his phone. He stands up.

"Don't look so shocked. I had a meeting nearby, so I came back for you."

"This is the first time you've ever driven me for an audition, so I think shock is the accurate feeling for me to have." I lean down to quickly scrawl my name on the sign-out sheet, then put my arm around his waist. "But I'm happy to see you, if that helps."

We walk down the long hallway toward the front entrance. "It does help," he says. "How did it go in there for the callback?"

I can't help smiling. "Really good. The director was there, and she said I've got a quality they are looking for."

"Cheezy?"

I hold the door open for him and then fake slam it in his face. We both laugh. The sun is shining and my spirit soars as we join the throng of people on the pavement. Every so often the thought, "You are a working actor," pops into my head, and I feel flushed from head to toe with pride. It's been an uphill battle with Val and Ed up to this point, but maybe somehow my luck is changing. Maybe they won't split up, and everyone will end up better as a result of this rough patch. Cole won't move to Calgary, Tim won't be so afraid, Butch will be healthy, and my parents will care that I'm succeeding as an actor.

Edward gestures down the street to a fancy coffee shop. I'm about to ask again if he'll help me with Ms. Kuntz when his phone rings. He fishes it out of his pocket and shows me the screen. Val. I look at him and try to communicate on an energy level that he shouldn't answer it. I have that sense of foreboding

JAMESY HARPER'S BIG BREAK | 123

that Val always seems to bring lately.

He pushes the green button and brings the phone to his ear. "Hi Val."

The expression on his face tightens up. "Slow down. Tell me again." People are rushing around us on the sidewalk, but they fade away. Everything shrinks down to Edward. As he listens, he reaches out to pull me close to his side. I move up on my tiptoes to try to hear what's going on.

"I'm with Jamesy right now. I'll bring her and find you. It's going to be okay." I can hear her high-pitched voice, frantic through the phone, but her words are indistinguishable. He murmurs a few more meaningless phrases, then hangs up. He turns toward me. I can see in his face that the news is going to be bad.

"It's Butch. He slipped in the shower and the doctor says his hip might be broken." I feel light-headed, with sparkles at the edge of my vision.

"He's not dead, right? He's alive?"

Edward pulls me into his chest, supporting me with his arms. His blue dress shirt is scratchy against my skin. "Of course he's alive. Your mom was upset, so it was hard to understand exactly what's going on, but why don't we go to the hospital now to get some answers."

I don't want to let go of him. If we stay here, I won't have to see Butch with a broken bone. If Val hadn't called, it never would've happened. Everything would still be okay. Butch would be playing cards at Sunny Acres, thinking about his evening glass of red wine.

Edward squeezes me one more time, then steps back to look at me. I don't realize I'm crying until he fishes in his work bag for a tissue. He puts his arm around me and we head to the car.

Monday, May 13th

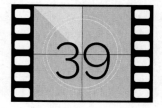

"They think he fell because a mass is growing by his knee. That's why he had that bump on his leg a few weeks ago." We sit in a soulless hospital waiting room. Ed has his arm around Val's shoulders and Tim huddles against Ed. I sit across from them, my arms folded across my chest.

"Didn't they biopsy the spot?" Edward asks. "When he was in the hospital before?"

Val nods. "The results were inconclusive. I hoped that meant no cancer. But now the doctor says the tumour could be growing so they'll biopsy it again and come up with a treatment plan. After the hip is repaired."

Butch has been in surgery for the last hour. Apparently, the hip isn't badly broken, just bruised with a fracture they wanted to stabilize in the O.R. He'll need to rest it (which he'll hate) but it's not too serious from what I can gather from the medical mumbling we heard from the doctor. The whole thing about the cancer/mass/tumour is much scarier. My brain is having trouble registering this possibility. I keep trying to wish my way out of it. Tim looks like he's using the same strategy, with his eyes tightly closed like he's pretending he's not even here.

My phone buzzes, and I try to look at it without alerting my parents. I've been texting with Cole, and he offered to come this evening, but I told him not to. Val's a mess, and something tells me I should stay here with her. The person I want the most right now is Butch, and I can't have him.

> Let me know what I can do. Ma wants you to come over when you can. And I want you too. So much.

My breathing slows down and catches in my throat. (Jameson, now is not the time to be a horny toad. Stop daydreaming about his gentle hands, his faint cinnamon smell, and the enticing idea that he wants me as much as I want him.)

"Jamesy?" I look up to see all three of them watching me. I slide my phone back under my leg. "Do you want to go home with your dad and Tim?"

"Are you going home?"

Val shakes her head. "I'm staying here until he's out of surgery."

"Then I'll stay with you."

Tim and Edward come to their feet. Edward says, "There's not much you can do right now, James. It might be a while and you've got school tomorrow. I'll be at the house with Tim until your mom gets home."

"I'm staying."

It's clear Val doesn't have the heart to argue. Edward squeezes my arm and I give Tim a quick hug, which he resists. Val stands too and we watch them walk away.

Left alone with Val. Not sure what I was thinking. The hospital might be cleaning blood off this floor. I offer a small smile. "Want some coffee? I can get it for you." Val's face is scrunching up and moving around, like she's a wind-up toy that someone else has set in motion. Her mouth becomes a thin line. She turns away from me, weeping, holding herself around the middle like she's physically falling apart.

For a moment I have no idea what to do. It's strange to see her like this, so out of control and actually human. For the first time she reminds me of Butch. Seeing the resemblance disarms me. I step toward her and pat her back, like she used to do for me when I was little and having a tantrum. Her breathing sounds wheezy and heavy, like a person with asthma. She's still bent slightly at the waist, her hair masking her features, but I've never, ever heard the keening sound she's making.

After a long time, Val sinks into a nearby chair. Nurses and patients scurry past the waiting room we are in, but thankfully no one else comes in. I move to sit beside her, patting her knee instead of her back, so she knows I haven't left. Her hands are still over her face, and now her breath comes in those short hiccupy bursts that follow a crying storm. I spy a box of tissues on the coffee table and contort myself so I can slide it toward us with my foot.

The motion causes Val to drop one hand and glance at me. Her blue eyes are spiderwebbed with red lines and her cheeks are wet and rosy. I pull a few tissues out and hand them to her. She scrubs at her face, then slowly sits back in her chair and looks at me. I'm tempted to say something funny to lighten this moment up, but for once I ignore this impulse and just wait. Besides, what is there to say?

"Thanks for not leaving." Her voice wavers, making her sound unrecognizable. "I'm sorry to lose it like that, but suddenly it was all too much."

"I get it. We're all worried about Butch."

"It's more than Butch. It's your father, and Tim, and this awful tension between you and me." She leans forward, drops her wadded-up tissues, and grasps me by my shoulders. "We've got to fix this mess, Jameson. You want to be treated like an adult and have me really talk to you about what's going on, but I don't see you behaving like one. Now is the time to prioritize your family and your schoolwork, by focusing on your future, and leave the other stuff until things have calmed down. Please. I need this from you. So does Butch. And your dad. And Tim. Give us all a chance. Please. We need you back."

Her tears have started up again. I can feel her fingers digging into my upper arms. I think about Butch, unconscious in surgery somewhere down a hallway behind locked and sterile doors. I can see Tim, crying and huddling against my dad. Cole's face swims into my mind, and I can hear him telling me that Val and Ed's problems have nothing to do with me, but at this moment I can't begin to believe that's true. Suddenly, it seems like I can fix what's been broken, with one simple solution.

Calmly, I reach both hands up and pry Val's fingers away. I hold her hands on my lap, warming them up. "Mom," I say. "I'll do what you're asking. I'll take a break from acting and focus on my family. It's going to be all right."

She pulls me in close for a hug. I feel her body trembling. She smells like peach bodywash and fresh air. We stay fused as one person for quite a while, long enough for me to forget everything except for my mom and how it used to be between us.

"So I found myself saying I would quit. She wants me to focus on my grandfather, and on the rest of my family. Hopefully it's just for a short time. It seemed to be the right thing last night at the hospital." I bite the inside of my lip, playing for time by reaching for my water bottle and taking a long sip.

Mrs. Wu nods. She sends out a supportive vibe, which is why I decided to dodge Lawrence and Brooklyn and even Cole to pick at my lunch in the drama room. She's usually in here over lunch, setting up for the next class, and I need someone to tell me I'm not making the biggest mistake of my life. "I know this is rotten timing for you, with roles finally coming your way this spring, but it's important to remember that you have many years ahead of you for acting. Your mom needs you right now. Family is an investment worth making, Jamesy."

I draw a long, wavering breath. I attempt to smile. Tears are close by, but I'm determined to stop crying. Today is a new day, and I'm attempting to face this new reality with as much courage as I can drum up.

A light knock comes at the door. Both of us look up to see Cole, leaning against the brown metal doorframe, with a concerned expression on his face and a runaway piece of brown hair tumbling down his forehead.

"Am I interrupting?" Cole asks.

Mrs. Wu stands. "No. I've got to photocopy scripts before lunch is over. Come on in." I rise to my feet and reach out to her for a hug. We've never hugged before, but it's not stiff at all. She squeezes me on the shoulder. "You're going to be okay. See you later." She grabs a pile of papers from her desk and smiles at

Cole on her way out.

Without a word he crosses the room and folds me into him. I start crying, like someone has turned a spout, and we stand like that for a long time. Cole is stroking the back of my neck with one hand and squeezing my side with the other one. When the tears are gone and my breathing evens out, I notice that my heart is pounding and I'm amped up, like it's Christmas Eve. I'm so glad he's here and I'm not on my own. I wipe my snotty face on his shoulder. He laughs. I look at the clock and register that we have five minutes until the bell rings.

Grabbing Cole by the hand, I pull him into the corner of the classroom. We fall onto an orange beanbag chair, the most comfortable piece of cheap furniture on planet Earth. He pushes my hair back from my face, and I lean in to kiss him. It's so easy to lose myself in his warm, seductive mouth. Everything shrinks down and blows away from me, like dandelion fluff on a summer afternoon. As long as Cole stays with me, no matter what else happens I think I'll be okay.

Our kiss intensifies. My hand finds the waistband of his jeans. When he pulls back, he groans, tightening his hold on me in the beanbag. "Your fellow actors are going to get a real show if we don't stop this."

"Cole, you're not going to Alberta, are you? Please tell me you'll stay here. With me." The words fall out of me in a rush.

"Hey. Buddy. Don't worry about that right now. You've got enough going on. Tell me about Butch."

"I stayed with Val all night at the hospital. Around midnight he came out of surgery, but he wasn't awake when I had to leave for school."

"Did you sleep at all?"

"Not really." I look into his green eyes like I'll find an answer there. "But it's okay." I can feel my lower lip trembling, the way it did when I was a little kid ready to bawl over something.

Cole kisses me, as light as a breeze. "Jamesy. Let me take you home. You need sleep more than school."

I'm crying for real now. I seem to have no control over it. "No, I can't. I have work after school and then I'm babysitting Dylan."

He shifts me from his lap and stands up. "Come on. You'll

flake on all of it, sleep for a few hours, and then everything won't seem so shitty."

I take Cole's offered hand and he pulls me to my feet. All I want is Cole, so I follow him out of the drama classroom and to the parking lot.

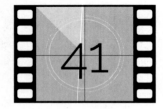

Cole tries to drop me off outside my townhouse, but I beg him to come up with me. "Hopefully no one's home," I tell him. "Ed will be at work, Tim has school, and Val should be at her preschool or at the hospital with Butch." I can read the indecision on his face. I squeeze his hand. "Please come in with me."

"If no one's home, I won't be able to control myself." Cole's voice is strained, like he's got a sore throat. I smile slowly at him, moving our joined hands to my chest.

"I'm counting on it," I say, kissing his fingers one by one. Hot damn! I feel bold and strong, like a sexy character in a movie. He pulls the car into an empty visitor spot.

I fumble with my key at the door while he kisses my neck. An old man walks his horse-sized spotted dog behind us on the tree-lined path. The dog barks at us. Finally, the key works and we fall inside. "Anyone home?" I call out, with my voice suffering from the same gauzy thickness as Cole's in the car. The only answer we get is a loud meow from Tubbs, who jumps down from Val's living room chair and stretches his front paws before coming to greet us.

"No one's here," I confirm, kicking my shoes off. I lock the door behind Cole and pull off his faded yellow T-shirt. He grins at me. I pull him by the hand, up the stairs, running down the hall to be sure we are alone. We end up in my room, a bit messier than I'd like for losing my virginity, but it wasn't like this was planned in advance. (Stop thinking about stupid shit, Jamesy. Focus on him.) Nothing else matters right now. We've waited long enough. I want him and I need him and everything's too much right now and he's here, so that's enough. Crockett tries to dart into my room, but I catch her and throw her back out, closing the door against future cat advances.

My breathing sounds heavy in my ears, as if I've been running for an hour. Cole's torso is smooth and toned, his nipples taut on his bare chest. His eyes look dilated, like he could be stoned. He stands in front of my bed, his jeans sitting low on his hips. Every one of my nerve endings is tingling, and I can't wait to touch him and have him touch me.

I unbutton my shirt, watching him. I drop it to the floor. I try my best not to worry about the fleshy part of my tummy or my hips. It doesn't seem to bother Cole, so maybe I should stop letting it bother me? He steps closer to me and I back up. I push my skirt down and step out of it, so I'm standing in front of him in my black bra and fuchsia panties. When he comes toward me, this time I don't move away. Our bodies merge into one another, my skin electrified by his. Our mouths are everywhere: lips, collarbones, shoulders, stomachs.

While he's kissing my ear and then my neck, I open my eyes for a second and see a framed picture on my nightstand of Val, Ed, Tim, Butch and me from last Christmas. We are all in matching pajamas in front of the tree, trying to hold onto two squirming cats. Everyone is laughing.

It's like cold water splashed onto my face. I feel disoriented, unable to concentrate. One of Cole's hands is in my hair and the other one plays with the waistband of my underwear. Suddenly, all I can hear is how hard both of us are breathing. "Wait," I hear myself saying. "Wait."

Cole takes one step back to look at me. His eyes are shiny, his lips damp. "What's wrong?" he asks in a whisper.

"I'm sorry. I want you so much, and we're finally alone, and everything was just right, but I saw this family picture while you were kissing me, and then I got worried about Butch all over again. I'm so sorry, Cole—"

He pulls me in tight against his body. "It's okay, buddy. Really."

My thoughts are all jumbled up in my head. I'm afraid he'll leave for Calgary and this will be my only chance for us to go all the way, but I don't want my first time to be when I'm scared and sad and distracted. It's confusing to want something so badly but at the same time worry that it might be too much, too fast. My fingers cling to him, like I used to hold on to my baby blanket.

"I'm sorry," I say again.

He leans back and pushes my hair away from my face. "Don't be. You're supposed to be sleeping, anyway. We'll find another time."

"Really? You're not mad?"

He smiles, then kisses me once, very gently. "No, I'm not mad."

"I love you, buddy." I swallow hard, flooded by relief.

"I love you, too. Now you really need to sleep." He finds my T-shirt on the floor and carefully pulls it over my head. I lift my arms and insert them one by one.

Cole pulls back my duvet and pats the mattress. I climb in and lie down.

"Are you leaving?" I hate how desperate that sounds, but it can't be helped.

"I'll stay until you're asleep, if you want, but I should go before anyone comes home." Cole covers me with the blanket, tucking me in, then he stretches out beside me. We hold hands. As I drift off to sleep, I feel safe and loved. My last conscious thought is that maybe everything will be okay after all.

I'm alone in a small corner of the school library, trying to finish math homework before the first bell. The numbers on the page in front of me swim and jiggle, making no sense at all. What I feel is Cole, deep in my cells. In my mind I can see us kissing frantically, his skin against mine, and imagine him lying beside me in my bed. School seems surreal by comparison. Because I've come closer than ever before to having sex, I can easily convince myself that I haven't quit acting, that Butch doesn't have cancer, that my parents aren't split up. Everything is like a bad dream except for Cole and me, and I can't stop imagining all that is still ahead for us.

"I thought I might find you here." I look up to see Brooklyn, clutching a box of Timbits. "In drama Lawrence told me about Butch breaking his hip. How is he?"

She sits down and opens the box. I gather my thoughts together, trying to remember how much Brooklyn adored Butch when we were little. If he bought me a treat, he got her one, too. Before he moved into Sunny Acres, we used to play cards with him at his house. He would pay us to mow the grass and weed his flowerbeds. Once a girl in grade two called Brooklyn an ugly Indian, and Butch hugged her while she cried, then offered to prepare a talk on racism and deliver it on a soapbox outside of the girl's house.

"He's had surgery for the hip but now they think he has cancer, which is why he fell in the first place. The doctors are running more tests to be sure, but he might have to have chemo. I don't even want to think about it."

Brooklyn leans over the table to squeeze my wrist. "That's

terrible. But he's the feistiest old guy I know, so if anyone can kick cancer's butt, it's your grandpa." She smiles.

"Thanks. That helps." I reach forward to grab a white-powdered Timbit with raspberry jelly inside.

Brooklyn tips her head and narrows her eyebrows. "Did something else happen? You look different to me." A million different responses fly through my brain. (Why yes, I got naked with Cole yesterday. You may have booked a film role before me, but in this area I think I might be first. Is it that obvious?)

I take a breath, lift up my phone to see the time, and close my binder. "Well, Val asked me to quit acting to focus on what's happening at home. She caught me at a bad moment, when Butch was in surgery, and I couldn't face fighting with her about school and auditions and everything. So I said yes. For now."

Brooklyn's voice is incredulous. "But you just started booking. You can't possibly quit now."

"I thought that too, but some things are more important." What I want to say but don't is that my parents won't drive me to auditions like hers do. My grandpa is the only family member who will chaperone me on set and now he's lying in a hospital bed while we wait to hear if he's got cancer. Edward has moved out of the house because he can't take the fighting and a big part of that fighting is my acting. If I stop, maybe I can fix this.

"Have you told your agent you're quitting?"

"I'm not quitting forever. Just taking a brief hiatus. It's not something you need to worry about." (Less competition for you.) I so badly want to say this, but I try to remember that we are inching our way back to friendship here. Best hold back my bitchy thoughts.

The bell rings and we both stand, gathering up our stuff. "Are you sure there's nothing else?" Brooklyn asks. "I can't put my finger on it, but something has changed."

We start walking toward the door. "I'm a day older now, Brooklyn," I tell her as we part ways in the hallway. "I'll never be young again."

I chuckle to myself as I head to science, imagining what she's going to make of that.

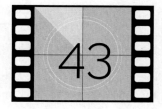

After school, the city bus has its usual four million people on it, so I'm standing somewhere in the middle, squashed between Lawrence on my left and a guy in his thirties wearing a torn Hawaiian shirt, who seems to believe that personal hygiene is optional. I'm on my way to the hospital and Lawrence is going into Vancouver to meet Darren at the art gallery for some travelling display of French painters.

"Is that what you gay kids are calling sex these days?" I ask Lawrence. "*French painters?*" He laughs, as I knew he would.

He puts on a campy accent. "Oh, darling, we would never be so tame."

The bus lurches to one side, preparing to take a corner, and my face swings dangerously close to Hawaiian Shirt's armpit. I clamp my mouth closed, waiting until the bus rights itself, then blow out my trapped air. "I might be experimenting with the ole French paint myself. Or getting closer, anyway." I grin at him. He shoves me with his shoulder, not willing to risk letting go of the bus strap near my head.

"You traaaaaaamp. I love it. Tell me everything." Hawaiian Shirt Guy turns his head toward me, clearly eager for details. Lawrence cracks up. "As fun as it is to entertain this bus with your wild ways, perhaps we should wait."

I don't even want to see if our unshowered friend is disappointed. "A solid plan. Anyway, the paint is, uh, still quite wet." In my head, this sounded clever, not dirty, but Hawaiian Dude raises his wild eyebrows at Lawrence and they fist-bump each other. I can feel my face turning fire-engine red, but anything I say to try to fix this will only make it worse.

My phone bleeps and I maneuver it out of my back pocket. It's Sam, my agent.

> Hey you! Great news! You BOOKED the MOW role. Congrats, Jamesy!! I'm lining up an audition on Friday for a car commercial. Amazing!

I'm hit with a stomach cramp. Oh, God. What now? Sam has worked so hard for me, with no pay in sight, and now that she's earning some commission, I'm backing away to keep Val calm and sane. I can feel myself starting to panic.

"What's going on?" Lawrence tips his chin toward my phone. "Hook-up invite?"

I shake my head, stuffing my phone back in my pocket. "It's my agent. I booked that movie-of-the-week role."

"Since you look like someone died, I'm guessing this isn't good news? After school television flicks aren't exactly my thing, but it pays, right?"

The bus stops and Hawaiian Shirt Guy lumbers to the back and gets off. Finally, a bit of breathing space that doesn't smell like ass. "It's Val," I attempt to explain. "She asked me to stop acting for now, to focus on Butch and the family and school. In a moment of high drama, I agreed, but now I have no idea what to tell Sam. 'I quit, for now' doesn't sound great out loud when I'm actually getting roles."

"Agreed. You sound like you're off your nut. Since when do you listen to Val, anyway?"

I bite the inside of my cheek until I taste blood. I can't keep arguing with my friends. Why can't I get even an ounce of goddamned support right now when I really need it?

Lawrence leans in closer, making a face at me. "Hey. Cheer up. I just don't see you as a quitter, but you'd better call your agent and talk to her about this. Don't text her. Ask yourself: WWJD?"

"What would Jesus Do?" I ask, baffled.

"Julia!" Lawrence answers. "My pretty woman would call her agent and explain. That's all I'm saying."

I'm laughing as the bus pulls up to the hospital. Lawrence salutes me as I make my way down the steps, and as the doors close, I can hear him yelling, "WWJD!"

"I'll take more of the kung pao chicken if Tim hasn't inhaled it all." Butch leans across me on his bed to grab for the take-out container. His left leg is elevated, resting on several pillows. Butch raises his eyebrows at Tim, who surrenders the box without a fight.

We're waiting for Butch's new biopsy results. Everyone is just a skitch tense. Ed's working late, Val is organizing Butch's cards and flowers, and Tim's face is pinched and tight. The only one who seems calm is Butch, but he's cheerier than usual, which is putting the whole room on edge.

I've been texting with Cole, who keeps finding inventive ways to say how much he misses me (my favourite: "like Venus de Milo pines for limbs"). Bantering with him keeps my mind off Sam, who texted again to be sure I got her message about the romance MOW. I send back a thumbs-up, but decide to wait until I have some damn clue what to tell her.

"Jameson, can you help me over here?" Val inquires. I stand up, put my phone down, and cross the small space to where she's stacking cards. "Can you look through these and see if we should keep some of them? I want to be ready to take him home as soon as we get the green light."

I take the cards and nod. "Did you go to work today?"

"No. I stayed here in case the doctors had something to tell me." Her words are clipped and forced. It's no use trying to jolly her along when she's this worried. I simply don't have the energy.

I put the cards down on my chair and go over to peer into the carton of kung pao. "I guess you've polished this off," I say to Butch, "with zero consideration for the hungry children in the room."

"Lying in bed with a bum hip works up quite an appetite." He hands me the box. I offer it to Tim, who shakes his head. I gather up the remaining containers and put them in the bag, then I hand out fortune cookies.

"Read them out loud," I suggest. "We need lots of good news."

A light knock comes from the metal door. I turn to see Cole, in a pair of navy shorts and a grey striped T-shirt with Bob Ross's face on it. I can't breathe for a second, looking at him. He holds up a backgammon board. "I thought Butch might like a game."

"He's not up to that right now." Val's tone verges on rude, and I think about Cole's mom getting up at four a.m. to drive me to set when I worked background.

Cole lowers the board. "No problem. It was just an idea." I walk over to him and take the game.

"You are so kind, Cole." I turn to Butch. "Wanna play, old man?"

He smiles at me. "I think your mom's right. I wouldn't be able to concentrate right now. But later on, I'd be happy to play. Thanks."

I take Cole by the hand and pull him closer to Butch. The air is friendlier in this section of the room. It's obvious Val doesn't want Cole around. My good intentions where she's concerned start to bleed away from me. We stand next to Tim and Butch for a few minutes, talking about nothing. Cole's thumb makes circles on my hand, driving me to distraction. I inch closer to him, so there's no space between us.

"It's getting late," Val announces. "I've got to get the kids home for school in the morning. I guess we'll have to wait until tomorrow to get any results from the doctors."

Cole turns toward Val. "I don't mind taking Jamesy and Tim home, if you'd like to stay."

Her voice is as frosty as the air conditioning. "I don't think that's a good idea. You're about to graduate, so you must have better things to do than spend time with kids in grades ten and six." (COME ON. Real nice and subtle, woman.) I experience an overwhelming urge to start screaming in her face about how I've almost had sex with this guy and when someone grows boobs and gets a monthly period, they should no longer be referred to as a "kid."

Cole squeezes my hand, keeping me from my planned tirade. "I don't have anything else to do. It would be my pleasure." He smiles, staring her down. We all wait. My breathing comes in short bursts. I know I'm going to utterly lose my shit if Val says no.

After what feels like an eternity, she nods. "I really do want to wait for the doctor to return. A ride for both of them would be helpful."

"No problem," Cole says. I release his hand, which I have been clinging to, and kiss Butch goodbye. He knows I'm upset, but Val is his fucking daughter. I can't say anything to him or this situation is going to spin further out of control. Tim hugs Butch and the three of us scurry out of the room, no one acknowledging Val at all.

"What the hell, jackass, I thought we were on the same team?"

"Not if you play like an old man. I'm miles ahead of you!" Tim twists and turns on the couch with his Xbox controller, like he's being chased by wild dogs. I'm trying to lean against Cole's shoulder, but he keeps inching forward, getting more and more into their war game and the trash talk that goes with it. I like seeing Tim relaxed. Cole's great with him. He's told me more than once that he's always wanted a little brother.

I stand up, collecting chocolate bar wrappers and empty root beer cans to take upstairs to the kitchen. Cole takes one hand off his controller to brush my calf as I walk away. I smile at him, hoping we can swing some alone time when Tim goes to bed, before Val or Ed comes home.

When I get to the kitchen I sit at the table, pull Crockett onto my lap, and dial Teresa. She answers on the first ring. "Jamesy? I thought Cole was coming to see you at the hospital?"

"He did. Then he drove Tim and me home because the damn doctors still didn't give us any news about Butch's biopsy and Val wanted to stay with him." I pause for a second, running my fingers around Crockett's velvet ear while she purrs like a jet engine. "Now they're playing Xbox, and I wanted to ask your advice on something."

"Sure," Teresa says. "Fire away." I tell her about booking the TV movie part, and Val's ultimatum, and not wanting to disappoint Sam, who worked so hard for me this past year. I'm sure it comes out more garbled than I want to sound, but my mind is racing, and I'm desperately hoping she'll be able to give me some idea of how I should handle this.

When I run out of steam, Teresa asks, "Would it help if I came to chaperone again on the days you work? Would that at least get you through this immediate crisis and you can see how Butch is doing after you finish shooting? Maybe things will change with Val and she won't hold you to this."

I let out the breath I've been holding. "I don't think Val is going to loosen up. And it's more than just Butch—it's also Ed leaving and them fighting. I've got to try to do what she wants, to see if it helps. It's got to." My voice cracks on the last word. I'm so fucking sick of crying. I refuse to do it, so I hold in the tears until my throat aches.

Teresa doesn't speak for what feels like forever. I brace myself, expecting the worst, but when she starts talking her voice is as gentle as a warm bath. "Maybe texting isn't the way to communicate with your agent. You might feel stronger and better about everything if you are brave enough to call her and talk about it. Tell her what you just told me. Use this as a practice for Sam. Can you see yourself doing that?"

I draw a long breath and visualize dialling Sam like I called Teresa. I feel calmer and just a bit more confident in myself. "I think I can do that tomorrow," I answer. "Thank you. Really."

Her smile comes through my iPhone. "Anytime, Jamesy. I'm here to help." Now I grin, sitting with my cat shedding all over my jeans, listening to my boyfriend and my brother click their controllers and shout over one another. "Are you still coming to Cole's commencement on Saturday afternoon?"

I feel cold all of a sudden, as the goofy happiness of making a decision and being cared for disappears like mist. Cole graduating means his dad coming into town to convince him to move to Calgary. Oh God oh God oh God. I can't think about Cole leaving me or I really will lose it. "Yes, I'll be there," I squeak out, hoping my voice doesn't sound as wimpy to Teresa as it sounds to me.

"Good," she says. "I'm looking forward to seeing you. I hope my Cole is behaving himself with you and being a gentleman." An image flashes through my mind of us upstairs in my room, his hands and mouth on me.

"Of course." My throat feels dry. I stand up, dump Crockett

off my lap, and pour a glass of water from the fridge. Teresa says goodbye and I see it's already ten thirty. "Time to go to bed, Tim," I call down the stairs. He starts groaning and complaining, but the sooner we can get him to bed, the quicker I can have Cole all to myself.

Thursday, May 16th

"Come on… Jamesy," Lawrence says between puffs on his vape while simultaneously making out with Darren. "Cowardly… is not a… good look on… you."

I stand by the smoke pit at lunch with my phone in my hand, watching Lawrence wrap himself around Darren. Part of me thinks they are utterly adorable, but the other part really wants Lawrence to pick one single activity instead of three different things at once.

"'Cowardly' is a bit strong, isn't it?" They continue slobbering all over each other, then finally Lawrence pulls himself away enough to talk to me.

"Look at me, out there and loving it with my new boyfriend. That's braver than you telling your agent you want to quit."

"For the millionth time, I'm not quitting, I'm just taking a short hiatus."

Lawrence takes a drag of his vape pen while fending Darren off with the other hand. "Just do it already, J. Right now, before we march to our deaths back to class."

My phone buzzes in my hand and I glance down to see Val's name. My insides twitch, but I tap the screen to read it anyway.

> Some of Butch's results came back but doctors say he needs a few more tests. ☹ Hopefully we'll know more soon.

Someone calls out to Lawrence, and he and Darren move as one unit farther away from me. I take a deep breath and pull Sam's number up on my screen. I wish I didn't feel so conflicted. I have no clear sense that this is right anymore, but

JAMESY HARPER'S BIG BREAK | 145

every time I consider doing this MOW role, I think about Val's disappointment, Edward's sadness, and Tim's tense face. I hit her number, exhale slowly, and bring the phone up to my ear.

"Jamesy, hi! How are things?" Sam's voice sounds bright.

"Hi Sam. I'm not great, actually."

"Oh no! What's wrong?" She sounds surprised, but also concerned.

I take a deep breath and plunge in. "It's amazing that I booked this TV movie role and I know you've worked so hard for me. All of those auditions with nothing to show for it but then the *Code Breakers* part and now this. I want to work, really I do, but the problem is my mom. She's never been happy about my acting, but she's seriously pissed about it now." I take a second and swallow hard, building up my courage. "We just found out my Grandpa Butch might have cancer and he's been in the hospital for a broken hip. And my parents are fighting and my dad moved out for a while. My mom asked me to focus on school and family and stop acting for a while."

"What do you want to do?" Sam asks after a short pause. "If we take your mom and your grandpa and your family stuff out of this, would you say yes to this role?"

"Yes." I have no hesitation. "Of course I'd do it, but it's not about me."

"I disagree. I think we can find a way to work this out, even with what everyone else needs from you. We have to try. These acting opportunities are hard to come by, and you've worked so hard to get here."

I can feel the pull toward Sam and away from Val. This is why I was afraid to call her. What she's saying is what I've been saying for the last year and a half. Fighting for the chance to prove I've got what it takes. And now it's here, my big break, and I'm turning it down like an utter moron.

My silence drags on between us. Tears are pooling in my eyes. I don't trust myself to speak.

"Jamesy, I think we should talk about this in person. Where are you right now?"

My voice is thick, like I'm pushing it through wet paper towels. "At school."

"When are you out? Can I come see you after school?"

"The bell rings at two forty-five. I was going to walk up to the thrift store because my boyfriend is graduating on Saturday, and I need to find a dress."

"I'll pick you up and take you there. Don't make any final decision until we've talked this through. I think we can find a way to make it work. I'm in this with you. I'm on your side."

I sniff loudly, thinking about Teresa telling me she's there for me anytime. Why is it so much easier with other people than with your own family?

"Okay," I say. "Thank you."

"Oooh, I found it! This is the one!" Sam holds up a stained off-white rag that looks like a woman may have been murdered in it (or really loved eating burgers with loads of ketchup on her wedding day). Dress shopping with Sam has turned out to be ridiculous fun. She's twenty-five and so cool it almost hurts to look at her, with her choppy short black hair, Converse runners, artfully torn jeans and a beaded top that looks straight from the '70s. Sam's my new style icon.

"Seriously, we have to focus," I say through the giggles. We're not getting far with the dress for Cole's commencement, but at least I'm not feeling the heavy dread that comes with disappointing my agent. All I want is a clear path forward where I don't have to upset anyone with my desire to be an actor—is that so impossible?

"Okay, okay. You start in this section at the mediums and I'll start in the larges and we'll meet in the middle when we've found the perfect dress. No more dicking around." Sam sounds mock serious. We both start moving the clothes, putting up with the screech from the hangers on the rack and trying not to inhale the musty scent of other people's lives as we search.

I pull one long sapphire blue gown out to examine, but it's too formal for a Saturday afternoon event. Sam says, "I don't understand why you won't let me talk to Val for you. It's my job to be your advocate and it sounds like you need one with your mom right now."

"It won't help. I keep telling you. She's dead set against it, plus I can feel a fight brewing about Cole. I can't give him up, Sam. I can't. Something has to give, and I know it can't be Cole, so what am I supposed to do?" Now I'm crying again. Sam comes quickly toward me and wraps me up in her arms. She rocks me gently, like a baby with a case of the farts, and for a moment it all fades away and I feel safe and cared for.

"Oh Jamesy. I'm sorry it's so shitty for you right now. It's really not fair." When we pull apart, she gives me a wry smile and I wipe at my damp cheeks. Sam turns her head to the side and gasps. "Look at this one!" She parts the rack where we are standing and pulls out a dress from the '60s with a brash pattern in peacock colours. Instantly, I fall head over heels in love with it. "Go try it on and I'll find you some gorg shoes."

She shoos me to the changing room and marches in the direction of the shoe rack. I pull the dingy plastic shower curtain across the wobbly pole and proceed to play the thrift store game "Don't let any item of clothing or your bare feet touch the manky floor." I pull the peacock dress over my head, begging the universe to let it fit. Balancing on the top of my Keds, I shuffle backwards and then look in the mirror.

The square neckline is white with a black line around it before the turquoise begins. The sleeves go just below my elbow, with a flared cuff and the same white and black trim as the neck. A paisley print is splashed here and there on the main body of the dress, which seems to hug me in the right places while being loose and comfy around my hips. It stops just above my knees. It looks like this dress was sewn for me sixty years ago, to wear to my boyfriend's commencement. I glance at the price tag: nine dollars. My heart swells up with happiness.

The curtain rustles. "Jamesy? How does it fit?" I inch out of the flimsy dressing room and Sam clutches at her heart like a proud grandparent. "It's divine," she breathes, holding up a pair of strappy white heels that are more '80s than '60s, but instantly I know they are perfect (and as a side benefit, Val will loathe them). Leaning on Sam's shoulder, I step into the shoes, buckle them up and admire the effect in the mirror. "Oh, to be sixteen again," Sam says.

We smile at each other in the mirror, and then Sam puts her arm around me. "Here's what I'm going to do about the MOW. I'm going to accept, on your behalf, because it won't shoot for a couple of weeks. Together, we'll figure out a game plan for upcoming auditions, Butch and his health, your family and their stuff. In the meantime, you'll go to this thing with your boyfriend on Saturday and knock everyone sideways in your '60s garb, and somehow, someway we'll get you doing this romance part when the time comes. And try not to worry so much. Okay?"

"What would I ever do without you, Sam?" I ask as we hug again. With Sam in my corner, I dare to believe that it might actually all work out.

"Well, I found you that smashing dress, so you certainly do owe me!"

Friday, May 17th

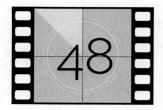

The Friday night crowd is settled in both cinemas, so Cole and I have a few minutes to ourselves. Grace isn't here, so the usual busywork of tidying the concession area can wait. I'm bursting to talk to Cole about Butch, Sam, the MOW role, Val's ultimatum, my call with Teresa, my gorgeous dress for his commencement tomorrow as well as regular boring school shit, but he's preoccupied. I hate that I feel a panicked tightening of my chest in these situations, but I always do. It makes me want to work harder to get him to be happy, but what am I supposed to do if it fails and then he's annoyed with me on top of everything?

He's fiddling with an empty pop canister. I move toward him and put my arms around his waist, leaning my face against his back, inhaling his light cinnamon smell. Cole squeezes my hands, then turns around to kiss me. His mouth is salty from the sour cream and onion chips he ate earlier.

"Hey buddy," I say when we pull apart. He smiles, but his eyes are far away. "Wanna talk about it?" I ask.

He steps back, shaking his head in frustration. "I don't even know what it is, so I'm not sure how to tell you about it."

"Okay. We can just hang out." I move beside him, leaning against the counter. Now we are both standing in a line, staring in front of us. Not weird at all. I'm not tense. (People say you should be comfortable with silence between you and the one you love, so this is good practice, right?!)

I can hear Cole breathing in and out, then he reaches for my hand. I bite my lip to stop myself from chattering and try to focus on waiting. Thankfully, after what feels like forever, Cole starts to speak. "I know I should be glad that I'm graduating, but I'm fucking drowning in finals and projects. I don't think I'm going to make it until the end of June. It's barbaric."

Cole sighs, running his free hand through his hair. I inch closer, pressing my leg up against his. I'm wearing a skirt and he's in shorts, so we are skin to skin. My pulse races, but I'm determined not to talk until I think he's run out of steam. "I wish I knew what I should be doing when I'm finally done with school. My dad's flying in tonight for the thing tomorrow, and I think we should talk to Mom about me maybe moving to Calgary to work with Dad for a while. But I know she'll lose her shit over that, so up to this point I've said nothing."

My heart starts drumming a steady beat of dread at the words "moving" and "Calgary," but so far I've done a marvelous impression of a supportive girlfriend, and I don't want to blow it now. But what will I do if he leaves? How do I breathe without him next to me?

Cole turns toward me, dropping my hand and using both arms to pull me in so our bodies are Velcroed together. He looks pained in this unflattering overhead concession lighting. "And then there's you. How am I ever going to leave you, buddy?"

I come up onto my toes and press my mouth to his, not the gentle kiss of earlier, but one much more urgent. I have to remind him of what it feels like when we are together. Like anything's possible. Cole's body is responding to me and our kiss grows in intensity, only breaking off because one of the theatre doors swings open for a mom and a young kid to scurry off to the bathroom.

"Come to Calgary with me," Cole says. "Is there any way that could happen?" I pause for a second, trying to imagine a scenario where this could work. Pros: No Val, Cole all to myself, a new city to explore, snow at Christmas! Cons: No Tim or Butch, no big film industry, still two goddamn years of high school to finish, cowboys, snow the rest of the winter.

His face holds so much hope, I hate to ruin this dream. "I'm sixteen. I don't see Val being enthused about sending me a whole province away. But if I don't act anymore, she might actually go for it." A lame attempt at humour, but Cole gives me a shadow of a smile. "And I couldn't leave Butch, not when he might be really sick. Or Tim, with my parents on the verge of splitting up." I put a hand up and touch a stray lock of hair on his forehead. "But you moving away would crack my heart in two. I know that for sure."

Cole leans down to kiss me again, softly this time. Then he wraps me in his arms and we stand there for a long time, no closer to any type of a decision.

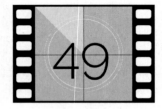

I'm putting on my makeup for Cole's commencement when Tim slides into my room, commando-style, on his stomach with his elbows alternating like pistons on the carpet. He's in his underwear, as usual. I turn my head slightly to the left, then return to my eyeshadow.

"You do know I can see you. Perhaps you'd better get your invisibility setting checked."

Tim dives into my double bed as if he's launched from a trampoline, snuggling under my duvet like he's done since he was little. "Can't you stay here today?" he asks, his voice muffled.

"Sorry, Timmy, Cole is graduating. I'd invite you but you'd hate it. Hours of names being called and polite clapping. You'll have to do it in two years for me and that will be more than enough for you."

I apply mascara to my eyelashes and glance at Tim in the mirror. He pulls the blanket down as he settles his head on my pillow. His hair is greasy and in need of a cut. He hasn't been showering and last night his light was still on when I turned mine off at midnight.

"It's all going to be okay. You know that, right? Worrying about Butch and the parents isn't going to change anything. We're both gonna be fine."

I finish with my mascara and put my makeup back in my dresser drawer. I sit on the bed and tickle Tim until he shrieks.

"Hey, that's too loud!" Val says from the hallway as she changes the laundry from the washer to the dryer. "Our neighbours are going to complain."

I offer Tim an exaggerated eye roll. I'm rewarded with a tiny smile. Val's footsteps warn us that she's coming, so there's enough time for Tim to pull the duvet back over his head. She stands in my doorway, looking me over with my hair styled and my makeup done. It's impossible to tell what she's thinking from her expression. I wish she would just say something nice, but I've learned that wanting that is a useless waste of energy.

"Can I see what you're wearing?" Val asks. I walk to my closet and pull out the hanger with my peacock dress on it, freshly washed to hopefully get rid of the earthy thrift store scent.

I hold it up against me and do a small pirouette. "Not bad for nine dollars," I say. I stare her down, daring her not to be flippant.

"It's a nice find," she responds. "I think it suits you."

I smile. "Okay, everybody out. I have to get dressed so I'm not late."

Tim scurries off the bed and out of the room, leaving a cloud of stink behind. Val waves her hand in front of her face. "Timothy Franklin! Get in the shower right now and put some deodorant on. Honestly!"

She steps out of my doorway and then turns back. "I know how important Cole is to you right now, Jameson, but he's in a totally different stage of life. I don't want you to get hurt. I'm just looking out for you."

I bite my lip, determined not to fight. I've got enough on my mind without debating Cole's age and graduation right now. All I have to do is wait her out. I stand in my robe, holding my dress and looking at her, until it becomes uncomfortable for both of us. "Okay," she finally says (because Val always needs the last word...and then the second last word too). "Please think about what I said."

I close the door behind her, put on my dress and my new white heels, then choose to put her out of my thoughts entirely.

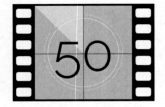

The noise in this auditorium is rising by the minute and the grads aren't even here yet. Each of the 375 grads gets four commencement tickets, but by the crowd milling around in here you'd think our high school graduates five thousand people.

I'm sitting with Teresa, her mother Nancy (who is basically deaf but the sweetest old person ever, who smiles all the time), and Bob, Cole's dad. He has longish sandy-blond hair and Cole's green eyes, like forest moss after a hard rain. He's as tall as Cole but leaner, probably from working outside as opposed to our cushy job at the Lantern. Bob's wearing a tie today, and he keeps pulling at his collar like it's choking him.

Teresa has already asked me about my discussion with Sam about the TV movie job, but I have managed to put her off the scent for now. The last thing I want to talk about on Cole's big day is Val and her interest in crushing my dreams. I told her I'm still trying to work everything out, which is utterly true, even if it doesn't get me any closer to an actual solution.

"I've sure heard a lot about you, Jameson," says Bob. "Cole's dated other people before, but not like this."

I smile and toy with the idea of saying thanks, but that doesn't sound right (plus, how many people has Cole dated exactly?!). "Well, the feeling's mutual. You've got a terrific son." Oh God, I sound like a boomer on a morning show. When I get nervous I don't sound like myself.

Teresa seems to realize that I'm tense. She leans over and squeezes my hand. "Can you join us for dinner after this? Cole wants to go to that Mexican place near the pier."

"Yeah, that would be great. Thanks for inviting me."

"Bob's only here for the weekend, so he'd like to spend as much time as he can with Cole before he goes home, but you don't mind, do you?" Teresa asks this in a pointed manner, hitting the words "only" and "goes" harder than the others. I've only spent fifteen minutes with both of them together, but it's easy to feel the underlying tension in the relationship.

"I'm happy for you to come along," Bob says. "It would mean a lot to Cole to have you there." This makes me think about Cole wanting to leave Vancouver for Calgary. The ache in my throat returns, making it hard to swallow. I look down at my phone to cover up this rising sadness, but my backscreen is Cole's grinning face, so it doesn't really help.

Thankfully, I'm saved by the first notes of Pachelbel's Canon. The crowd slowly settles down as the endless march of grads begins. We all watch for Cole, leaning forward in our seats. Finally, he appears, in his blue cap and gown, wearing the burgundy tie I bought for him as a grad gift. Is there any chance he's really moving away from me? I find it impossible to consider. My brain freezes, turning into a spinning rainbow wheel at the very idea.

When Cole's on the stage, in his seat, I watch him search the crowd for us. He looks so handsome that my heart constricts. I glance to my left at Teresa, who is tearing up already. Then I look to my right, at Bob, who is bursting with pride. Cole's granny is smiling exactly the same as always. I turn back to Cole and wait for him to find us in the middle of this massive auditorium.

When he sees me, his face melts into a grin. He raises his eyebrows three times, our code for "I love you." I mirror the gesture, wondering how much everything is going to change in just over a month's time.

Saturday, May 18th

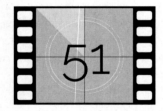

"To Cole," Bob says, with his bottle of beer in the air. We all raise our glasses for the toast, our faces rosy in the candlelight. I squeeze Cole's leg under the table and drink my virgin pineapple margarita with the other hand. Teresa smiles brightly, adding, "We are all so proud of you. We can't wait to see what you do with your future."

We are halfway through our meals at Cole's favourite Mexican place on the beach. I'm having chicken enchiladas with mole sauce and he's on his third steak fajita. Teresa took Nancy home after the graduation because she was tired (from smiling?), so now it's just the four of us. We're sitting on the patio and the sun is going down over the water. I try to pay attention to this moment because I want to remember it, but talking about Cole's uncertain future makes me feel instantly nervous.

"So what are you planning to do with your future, by the way?" Bob asks, before taking an enormous bite of his carnitas taco.

I freeze up. "There's loads of time to figure all of that out," I say, attempting to sound relaxed. "Right now we should celebrate."

"Hear, hear," Teresa seconds. Is it possible she's worried, too?

Cole puts his hand over mine, then says to Bob, "I do have one idea about my future, but it's complicated."

I swallow hard, then risk a glance at Teresa. Her eyes are wider than usual, and she starts biting her lip. My stomach drops like I'm on a scary ride.

Bob leans back in his chair. He wipes his mouth with his napkin. "Let's hear it."

Cole draws a deep breath, squeezing my hand. I feel like any motion I make will be interpreted as encouragement for this mad plan of his, so I try to remain still. The silence seems to go on for a long time, making an already sketchy situation seem downright ominous.

Finally, Cole starts to talk. "I'm thinking I could use a change. The last time I visited you in Calgary, I wondered what it might be like to live there for a while and maybe work with you in construction. Just until I figure out what I really want to do with my life. There's no point in applying to university and not having any idea what I want to focus on. I'm hoping I can figure that out if I give myself some time."

My eyes drill into the wood table. The noise of the servers bustling around and the other diners talking and laughing fades into a low hum.

"We've been talking about your future non-stop for the last year," Teresa says. "You've never once mentioned going to Calgary."

I can feel Cole turn to look at his mom. "I didn't know how to tell you. I thought you'd be upset."

"Well, you thought right." Her voice is shaky and low.

Bob says, "Hey, Teresa, that's not fair. You've had Cole to yourself for a decade now. If he wants to spend some time with me, let's not punish him for that. I think it sounds like a good idea." He turns to Cole. "I'm sure I could get you work on my crew."

"Thanks Dad." I raise my eyes to Cole's face because I can't bear to look at Teresa. "Mom, nothing is for sure yet. It's just an idea. But I'd like to bank some money and take a break from school for a while."

"That's what the summer is for. Have some fun and relax. Plenty of kids figure out what they want to do in their first year of university."

Cole says, "I've missed the deadline already. It's too late for this fall."

"I'll do some research with you. Starting at a community college is a reasonable idea for someone with your grades. I was talking to Kevin Silver's mom and she said—"

"Mom, stop. Please. I don't need you to plan my future."

Now I look over at Teresa. She has tears in her eyes. It seems like I don't belong here at this dinner. I'm trying to get my legs to work in order to stand up when Teresa beats me to it.

"Okay, Cole, I won't. I'll say goodnight." She gathers up her purse and walks out of the restaurant. Cole sighs loudly, shaking his head. Bob takes another bite of his taco. I stay quiet and still, wishing I could disappear without anyone noticing.

Sunday, May 19th

Butch is back at Sunny Acres, settled into his bed with his hip elevated by pillows. I spent most of the day at home, besieged by homework and trying my best to forget about Cole leaving and Teresa crying last night, but now we are here in Butch's tiny room for dinner. Val finishes fussing around with her crockpot chili and comes over to the bed.

"Before we eat, I have some news from the doctors that we should discuss," Val says. I add a few emojis to my text to Lawrence and put my phone away. I'm sitting by Butch's feet on the bed. Tim is on Ed's lap in the recliner. When I start to feel faint, I realize that I'm holding my breath. I breathe in with a sharp sound and Butch nudges me with his foot and smiles.

"Don't look so worried," he says. "I'm a tough SOB, you all know that."

Val appears strained (but there's nothing she likes so much as commanding a room with her voice). "It's taken a while for the doctors to give us a diagnosis, because something was wrong with the first biopsied sample, but now they think they know what caused Butch to fall in the shower. He has a small tumour growing by his knee. It's called soft tissue sarcoma."

Tim's eyes have gone wide. "What does that mean?"

"It means cancer." My voice comes out louder than I wanted, my throat scratchy and dry.

Butch reaches out a hand to grab for Tim's. "It's not that serious, Timmy Bear. My doctor says it's low-grade, which is the best kind of tumour to have in your leg. It's not good for my soccer career, but I've been thinking of quitting that anyway."

None of us laugh at Butch's stupid joke. I turn away from Val and look at Butch. "Can't they take it out with surgery?"

He opens his mouth to answer but Val beats him to it. "Not right now. It's in a complicated spot, wrapped around his ligaments by the knee, so first they want to do some radiation to shrink it. Then maybe chemo. But it's all going to be fine. Nobody should be worried."

I bark out a strained laugh. "Yeah, that's how it works. 'Don't worry, everyone. It's just cancer in a seventy-four-year-old guy. NBD.'"

"Take it easy, Ducky," Butch cautions. I close my eyes, concentrating on breathing in and out so I don't start screaming or breaking shit. I don't want to look at Tim, who must be freaking out. I can hear him crying softly, with Ed and Val fussing over him, making soothing noises.

"Jamesy. Come here." Butch's voice is soft and quiet. I open my eyes, flooded by tears, and see him gesturing to me. Carefully, I climb toward him, taking care not to bump his injured hip. He moves his arm to the side to make space for me. I curl up to him like I'm five years old, my head tucked under his chin. This is why he calls me Ducky, because when I was little, I curled up like a duckling in Butch's feathers, protected and safe from anything that could hurt me. And now he has cancer.

It's all too much. I can't bear any more uncertainty and loss. I haven't got acting to look forward to. Cole is probably leaving. Ed might move out for good, leaving Tim and me alone with Val. And now Butch, the person I rely on the most, could die and leave me in a world I cannot imagine without him in it. The sobs come, one after another, like waves. My body is racked by them. Butch pulls me in even tighter. I can smell the spices in the chili. I cry until there's nothing left inside of me and I'm empty, like a room that's been swept clean.

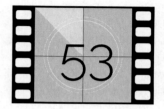

"I know your life's a fucking shitshow and everything, but are you going to eat the rest of your pancake?"

"Jesus, Larry, you just ate a full hearty breakfast, the biggest thing on the menu, and you still want my banana chocolate chip pancakes?" Lawrence takes a long drink of his cupcake milkshake (possibly the most disgusting thing I've ever tasted), reaching slowly for my plate. I slap his hand so violently the syrup caddy rattles.

"Fine. Be that way. I guess I'm getting kind of full anyway."

I roll my eyes at him, but I can't help smiling. Lawrence drives me up the wall, but he's an excellent distraction on this holiday Monday morning (Happy Queen Victoria's Birthday Day). He texted me last night, just before my emotional collapse on Butch's bed, to ask for a bistro breakfast to talk about Darren.

"So what should I do?" Lawrence asks.

"Just tell your mom," I suggest. "She's likely to take it better than your dad."

"No shit. But telling her is telling him because he's 'the head of the house' and basically God, according to the fucking Bible. My Dad's already threatened military school and I'm not cut out for that scene. They'd eat me alive."

"I don't think you can have cupcake milkshakes in the military." I make a face at him, to try and lift his gloom, but he sighs loudly.

"We spend so much time over at Darren's because his parents are cool with us being gay. It's no big deal to them. Darren thinks I have to tell my parents for my own sake, no matter what happens, but somehow I can't bring myself to ruin my dad's idea of me. I know this makes me pathetic."

He's so sad that my heart squeezes in my chest. I cut off a section of my last pancake and dump it on his empty plate. "Here. Because I love you."

Lawrence stabs at it, playing with the banana slices on top. "Of course it doesn't make you pathetic," I say. "It's your parents who are wrong. You and Darren are the cutest couple, and it's a crime to deprive themselves of the pair of you. But coming out to your parents is a huge deal, and you should only do it when you are ready." He looks up, a tiny bit of hope in his brown eyes.

"Thanks. Maybe I'll never be ready." Lawrence shrugs, then cuts off a section of my pancake and shoves it in his mouth. "What are you gonna do about your man?" he asks while chewing.

Now it's my turn to sigh. "There's nothing I can do. He wants to go. His mom is pissed and I'm crushed, but Cole wants to leave BC and try working in construction with his dad. I can't exactly make him stay."

"You can turn up the heat for Sexytown." He says this just as our waitress, Mildred, comes by to drop off our bill. Mildred smirks at Lawrence (she might be ninety, but ole Mildred knows what's up). Lawrence puts two fingers on the bill and slides it dramatically across the table to me.

"Sexytown notwithstanding, I've also got Butch and Tim to think about. Cole asked me to go with him to Calgary, but I can't just take off with two years to go for high school. I wish so bad I were in grade twelve with Cole, and then we could leave together."

"And I wish I were straight and manly enough to satisfy my parents, but they're stuck with my queer ass and you're fucking stuck in high school with me for an eternity." He pulls his old-school camouflage Velcro wallet out of his pocket and throws down a five-dollar bill for the tip. "Besides, maybe Cole won't go. If he spent all day yesterday with his dad, maybe they had a fight or Cole realized he wouldn't want to live with him. Dads really aren't that great."

I picture Edward, then Larry's dad, and then Bob. Ed used to be great, but what is it with dads as their kids get older? It's like they want us to stay little and innocent forever. "I have to babysit Dylan after this but tonight I'm going to a grad party at Big Dave's with Cole, so I'll find out if your dad theory is right or wrong."

I really hope it's right.

Goddammit, Lawrence was wrong. Cole's in a great mood, drinking with his friends and pulling me up to dance with him when a decent song comes on. I wanted him to say that after spending a day alone with Bob he can't imagine leaving Teresa and moving to Calgary, but it seems like they had a ton of fun hanging out together. I'm happy to see Cole blowing off some steam and relaxing tonight instead of stressing out over his upcoming finals and projects, but cold fingers of dread are inching around in my gut.

Cole puts an arm around my waist and pulls me close. We kiss, long and hard, while other sweaty bodies crowd around us in Big Dave's living room. "Almost there!" someone shouts over the music, while a few people respond, "Fuck high school!" and "Finally!" One day it will be my turn to celebrate graduating, but not for two long years, so my predominant feeling is one of jealousy at this moment.

The song finishes, and a new one starts blaring. Cole and I move apart. Someone turns the sound up even higher. Big Dave comes over to Cole and slaps him on the back. They start shouting at each other, over the music, and I gesture toward the kitchen. Cole lets go of my hand and I thread my way through the crowd, looking for a quieter place to collect my thoughts. The kitchen isn't much of an improvement, with people playing beer pong and other sloppy drinking games. I grab a can of lukewarm Pepsi from the counter and step outside onto Big Dave's patio. The music is still thumping away out here, but it's muted, and that's exactly what I'm looking for.

Away from noise and people, Sam rushes into my mind. I

remember our day shopping at the thrift store, when she offered to talk to Val with me about the movie-of-the-week job. Oh shit, she's accepted that on my behalf, which means any day now I'll get wardrobe fitting information and a call date to shoot. Then I'll have to face Val or turn it down. Sam reminded me recently that this will be my second professional credit, after *Code Breakers*, so I'll only need one more to apply for full union status. Once I get three credits, I'll be paid union rates for all work in the future, which equals a decent chunk of change toward my university account. A year ago, joining the Union of BC Performers with three credits was my biggest dream. And now I'm days or weeks away from my second TV credit, and I'm considering saying no?

Well, now I'm crying again. Everywhere I turn with my thoughts, I hit a dead end. Maybe what I need most, like Larry Boy, is courage. To face up to what I really want and be willing to ride out the storm when other people don't want me to have it. So what do I want? Number one, to act. To chase this big dream and go for it no matter what. Number two, to stay in love with Cole and have him stay in love with me. Key word there is "stay." Number three, for Ed to move back home and for us to be a family again. And, of course, number four (which is actually number one), for Butch to be healthy and alive and there always at Sunny Acres. If only I knew how to make these things happen, even just a few—

"Buddy." Cole is beside me, looking right at me, and I have no idea how long he's been there. He sets down his beer and wipes the tears from my cheeks with his thumb. I notice his green eyes in the twilight. The yard smells like grass, flowers, and soil. Cole leans over to kiss me. He feels solid, warm, and dependable. When he pulls back, he smiles. "You know I love you, right?" he asks.

I don't think I can speak past the lump in my throat. I drop my unopened Pepsi and grab the front of his teal shirt with both of my hands, like I'm drowning and he's about to rescue me. "I have an idea," Cole says, his face an inch from mine. "Let's spend tonight like we have all the time in the world to be together. No talking about the future. Let's have a few drinks and imagine that we'll go on forever and nothing will change. You, me, the shitty Lantern Cinema, all of it. Deal?"

He tucks a strand of hair behind my ear. We look at each other for a long time. Someone screams from an upstairs window. The music stops for a moment, then starts up again. Laughter comes from the kitchen when someone wins at beer pong.

"Deal," I say.

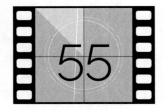

"I know you've all been eagerly waiting for the announcement of next year's musical, so here it is." Mrs. Wu pauses for dramatic effect. Brooklyn glances at me. I turn my head to look at Lawrence. We've been speculating for weeks (will it be *Matilda*? *Peter Pan*? *Chicago*? Likely not *Chicago*, as it's too racy for Mrs. Wu, but a girl can dream of a role like Roxie).

"It's *Kinky Boots*, isn't it?" Lawrence asks, getting the whole class to laugh. I can SO see him as Charlie Price.

"Next year, our musical will be… *Captain Fuzzy's Last Fight!*" I'm aware of my classmates gasping and chattering away to one another, but everything goes still for me. I can see myself on stage, as Captain Fuzzy herself, in all of her commanding feline military glory. I imagine belting out Fuzzy's final number, "And here, on this drenched battlefield, the torn bodies littered by my feet…"

Lawrence shakes my arm. "Captain Fuzzy, Bitch!" he shouts. I come out of my imaginary stage trance to see Brooklyn looking at me. She's smiling, but I can see her Fuzzy wheels turning as quickly as mine are. This is going to be interesting.

"I'm expecting all of you to audition in a couple of weeks, before summer break. We'll have lots of roles to fill, and chorus members will be busy in this show." She's still talking, but I start obsessing instead of listening. Oh God, why am I thinking about playing Captain Fuzzy in my school musical when I can't even figure out how to get Val to let me act in the TV movie I've already booked? High school theatre doesn't pay anything and I need money for university, but I really want to be the lead in this show. Can I beat Brooklyn for the part? I think I'm a better actor, but Mrs. Wu might not agree. And the rehearsal schedule will be intense, which could make it hard to get to auditions and roles, provided I'm allowed to act in the first place without getting kicked out of my house —

"Hey," Lawrence says quietly. "Class is over."

I shake my head, like a wet dog, and turn to look at him. "Hope I didn't miss anything important."

"Nah." He stands up and pulls me to my feet. "And I thought I was preoccupied these days."

We both grab our bags and start walking out into the throng of humanity in the halls. "Is it Cole leaving? Or Butch? No wait, I bet it's the old standby, Val."

"Yes, yes, and yes. All of them. The last thing I need is to try to beat out Brooklyn for the lead, but I really wish it weren't *Captain Fuzzy's Last Fight*. Why couldn't it be a musical I don't care about?"

"'Cause you're not that lucky. None of us are."

We get to our lockers and start changing out binders. I take a moment to really look at Lawrence, noticing he has dark circles under his eyes. "No closer to telling your parents?"

He shakes his head, cramming a textbook into his messy locker. "I can't eat. I can't sleep. Not telling them is becoming worse than telling them, but I'm worried I'll just put it off forever because I'm a fucking coward."

I close my locker and turn to him, nudging him with my shoulder. "Hey. You are not a coward. Not even close. Stop it with that shit. When you're ready, you'll do it. Until then, please eat and sleep."

Lawrence smiles at me. "Okay. I have French next, so I'll sleep there." He flips his skate shoe up to tap me in the butt before heading down the hall. Halfway down he turns around, his books clutched to his chest, and salutes while shouting, "Good luck to you, future Captain Fuzzy!"

I laugh as kids bitch at him for disrupting the flow. The bell rings and I walk to math, bracing myself for the longest block of the day.

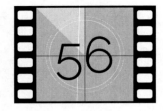

The flower gardens are so pretty at Sunny Acres. Two employees are down on their hands and knees in the beds, yanking out weeds and removing deadheads from the roses. Butch and I are strolling on the paving-stone path. He's using a walker (which he hates and keeps cracking jokes about) and is moving quite slowly because he had his first radiation treatment this morning while I was at school.

"You know you can always talk to me, right, Ducky? Holding your troubles in like this is not good for you." I wish it were as simple as telling him about Cole, and how I don't know what to do about this MOW part, and about Lawrence coming out to his parents who are likely going to freak out, and a whole bunch of other shit, but I can't do that to Butch right now. He comes first in this situation.

I look at Butch and smile. "It'll all work out, I'm sure. You have enough to worry about right now."

He stops and leans on the walker. "Jamesy. Talk to me. I held you when you were an hour old. I know something's wrong, and I want to hear about it."

My phone buzzes with a text. I pull it out of my jeans and look at the screen while gesturing toward a nearby bench. "Are you tired? Want to sit down for a second?"

"I don't need to sit down," Butch says. "I want you to tell me why you are so down lately."

The text is from Cole.

> Hey buddy. You're on my mind but I'm slammed
> with HW. I cannot wait to be done school. Less

than a month now. If I finish before midnight I'll call you. U ok?

(Hmm. Am I okay. No, not really, but how the hell am I supposed to answer that in a text? And it's great that you can't wait to be done school and it's over soon, but you're planning to leave for Calgary which kind of dampens my excitement for you.) I shove my phone back in my pocket without answering. I'm here to focus on Butch.

"Who was that from?"

"Cole." I want to say, "He's leaving me and I can't breathe thinking about him not being here," but there's no point. Complaining isn't going to change anything.

"You can text him back. Or call him. I don't mind." Butch's voice is gentle. I think of it as his "careful voice."

I swallow hard. "Nah. Let's keep walking and work up an appetite for the famous Sunny Acres tea. I hope they have blueberry muffins today."

We start shuffling forward again. "We had them yesterday. So today they will be stale."

"Delish," I say just as my phone rings. I grab it, hoping to see Cole's smiling face on my screen, but instead I see Sam. My stomach clenches. I go to stab at the decline button, but I'm stopped by Butch's hand on my wrist.

"Facing it is better than running away. Trust me on this, my Duck. You are more capable than you think you are."

Goddammit, now I'm on the verge of crying. I draw a long, quivery breath, while looking at Butch for courage, then hit answer.

"Sam?"

"Hi Jamesy! I've finally got news on the TV romance thing." She pauses. I watch Butch make his way over to the bench and sit down. "It's filming next week. Your part is scheduled for two days—Wednesday and Thursday. It's your second credit toward full union status, Jamesy. You are almost to three for a lot more money for future acting work, plus benefits and a matching RRSP. You told me when we met that this was your goal and you've worked so hard this year to make it to this point." It's obvious she's trying to convince me to do it, but I'm not the one who needs convincing. "You're going to do it, right?"

"Yes," I say with zero conviction. "I'll figure it out. Send me the details when you get them, and I'll make it happen."

She squeals in delight. Butch smiles at me. I feel like the walls are slowly closing in on me, and soon I'm going to be crushed.

I call Ed after school and beg him to meet me at the pub for dinner. I've reached the limits of what I can do on my own. I need his help. Tim really wants to come, but I tell him I need to talk to Edward alone. He's pissed, but I'll bring him back an order of dry ribs and he'll chill out.

Ed and I split a bunch of stuff on the happy-hour menu. Half-price hamburgers, yam fries, quesadillas, dry ribs, and chicken wings from three to six. Ed has a beer and I'm halfway through an iced tea. I've been making my case for the last thirty minutes, telling him about full membership in the union, how hard my agent has worked to get me in front of casting directors, how good I've had to be to beat out other actors like Brooklyn for these parts, and how much money I can save for college by working these jobs. I've laid my case out the best I can, and now I wait for Ed to tell me what he's planning to do about Val.

I dip another yam fry into the mayo aioli and stuff it in my mouth. "Please, Dad. I need you to talk to Val about this. I have to do this TV movie job on Wednesday."

"Between you and me, I think your mother is being too harsh with you about this. It was one thing when Butch was in the hospital and she was under a lot of stress, but he's home now, and I think she should ease up on you a little."

"Wow. I've never heard you go against her like that. It means a lot to me."

Ed sips at his beer. "I'm not sure it will help you for me to get involved. I'm worried I'll make it worse. As you know, things aren't exactly good between your mom and me right now."

I lean forward across the shiny table to pat his arm. "Thanks for actually being honest with me."

He nods, opening up a wet wipe for his chicken-wing hands. "I'm sorry, Skittles. I just don't think I can change your mom's mind. I think she'll be more open if you talk to her about it. With me it will become a fight in a hurry." His eyes cloud over. For a moment, he looks immeasurably sad. I decide to take it easy on him.

"Okay. Thanks anyway, for listening. I appreciate it."

He pulls out his wallet, preparing to signal our server for the bill. "I wish things were different, Jamesy. For all of us."

"Me too." As Ed pays, my phone chimes. I read this from Lawrence:

> I did it. I told them about Darren and now I'm utterly fucked. He gave me five minutes to pack a bag. I'm at Ginny and Ben's. Mom didn't say a single word.

Oh God. Ginny and Ben are Lawrence's aunt and uncle. They aren't much warmer than his dad, but at least they let him stay there.

I stand up with Ed, texting Lawrence with one hand as we walk out of the pub.

> I'm coming over. Don't do anything stupid and I love you. It's going to work out. xoxoxoxo

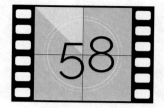

Lawrence is in his aunt and uncle's guest room. It's small, and overstuffed with terrifying dolls and knick-knacks (I think there are at least a hundred in here), but at least he's not under a bridge clutching a sleeping bag. He's sitting on the edge of the narrow double bed, with a lumpy mattress that sinks into the centre, staring into the middle distance.

Ed dropped me here after dinner. I endured a few minutes of stilted chitchat with Lawrence's aunt Ginny, who whispered in her entryway as if spies might be eavesdropping. She mentioned (I think?!) that Ben was watching baseball in the den so Lawrence and I should keep the noise down because Ben's hearing isn't very good. The TV is blaring nearby, so I'm not worried about us competing with that.

I walk into Lawrence's room and close the door behind me. He looks like a ghost. I carefully sit down beside him. He doesn't say anything and his breathing is shallow. After a few minutes, I say, "If you want to tell me about it, that's fine, and if you don't want to, that's cool, too. We can just hang out, or watch old eps of *Shameless*. Whatever you want."

We sit, shoulder to shoulder, and I try to focus on deep breaths, hoping that Lawrence will follow my lead. After what feels like an hour, he starts talking in a strange monotone, his eyes on the forest-green shag carpet. "It was just Mom and me for dinner. I thought she'd be able to handle it, so I told her that I was dating a boy. I said that I didn't know if I was gay, that I really liked this particular guy, but I also feel attracted to some girls. I hoped that might help, make her not worry so much." He's trembling, so I put my arm around his shoulder to try to steady him.

"She seemed to be listening. She didn't say anything, but I felt so relieved to have it out there in the open. When I ran out of things to say, she got up from the table, said 'Excuse me,' and walked out of the room. I should've left right then, but part of me was hoping she was just going to the bathroom or taking a minute to collect herself."

He trails off, still shaking. I can hear his teeth chattering slightly. "What happened next?" I ask.

"My dad burst in the front door. I tried to quickly stand up from the table, but he made it there so fast. He grabbed me by the shirt and threw me up against the wall. That pastel seaside picture my mom loves fell to the floor. I could hear her gasp, but she didn't say anything. He said a bunch of shit about how fags go to hell and that the Bible is very clear on this point. 'No son of mine will be this way,' he shouted at one point." I close my eyes, imagining Lawrence's dining room, with a growing sense of horror. "He dragged me to my room and stood in the doorway with his arms crossed over his chest. He looked huge. I had five minutes to pack some clothes and my phone charger. Then he grabbed me by the collar and literally threw me out the door into the rain, like you'd see in a movie. He slammed the door behind me, so hard the windows rattled, and turned the deadbolt."

"Oh my God. Larry. That's unbearably awful." I realize that he's crying, but trying to act like he's not, and I'm filled with a sweeping anger. How dare Frank do this to Lawrence, who is the sweetest and gentlest person ever? Why is it that some people who say they believe in a God of love act with so much hate?

"What about Darren? Do you want me to call him?" I ask. He shakes his head, gulping for air. "Okay. I get it. Come on, let's lie down and get you under this hideous bedspread from the Civil War era."

Lawrence doesn't move. I slide down to the carpet and take off his shoes, then I ease him backwards until he's lying down. I fuss around him with the blankets and the hard pillows, then lie down next to him. The bed is as uncomfortable as it looks, and it smells like dust. I put my head near his. He grabs for my hand and holds it with a tight grip.

There's no way I'm leaving him. I'll stay right here, for as long as he needs me.

Friday, May 24th

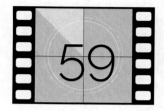

By the time I knock on Teresa's door at seven thirty p.m., I think I've formulated a workable plan. I don't realize how nervous I am until she opens the door and smiles at me.

"Aren't you supposed to be at work with Cole right now?" she asks.

"I called in sick."

She gestures for me to come inside. "Are you sick?"

I shrug, while kicking off my Keds. "Does stressed count?" Teresa's house is so welcoming. Why couldn't mine have this feeling of warmth and security in it?

"Sure. Mental health and all that." I look at her, in the spring evening light, and notice that she looks pale and tired. She must be thinking about Cole leaving for Calgary, just like I am.

"Did Bob go home to Calgary?" I ask.

"Yes," Teresa answers, her voice pinched. A small silence falls between us, and I remember her crying at the Mexican restaurant before she walked out.

"Can I get you something to drink?"

I shake my head. "I just want to ask you something. I think I've come up with an idea that will solve a few problems at once, but I need to know if it works for you."

"I'm intrigued," Teresa says. She leads the way into the living room, and she sits on the couch while I pull my legs up under me in the flowery wingback chair.

"Go for it."

I take a long breath to bolster my courage, then dive right in. My voice sounds shaky, and I have trouble making decent eye contact, but I just have to get this out and hope Teresa goes for it. "Okay. Here it is. Sam called and said the MOW part films next week, on Wednesday and Thursday. She accepted it for me ages ago, even after I told Val I wouldn't act anymore, when Butch was in the hospital with his hip. Sam kept saying I'd figure out a way to make it work, as it's my second credit toward full membership in the union and saying no is a bonkers idea when it hasn't even made Val any happier."

"Jamesy, I think—"

I wave my hand at her and continue. "Wait a sec. I just want to finish. So here's my idea. I don't want Cole to move away any more than you do, but I think it's happening anyway. I can't act and live at home with Val but when Cole goes, you'll be all alone here, and I was hoping I could move in here with you. Then I'll still be close enough to check on Tim and make sure he's okay, and ditto with Lawrence, and stay at school but go on auditions and work. And I can pay you for rent and maybe we won't miss Cole so much if we are together." I stop abruptly, with tears clouding up my throat, and I'm so afraid if she says no I'm going to panic and rush out into the street.

Teresa stands and comes over to me. She kneels down by my chair and folds me into a giant hug. She's wearing a soft pink hoodie, and the material feels comforting by my face. I cry for several minutes, loving the sensation of being held, and then finally pull away. I wipe my snotty nose on my sleeve and we both laugh at the mess. She gets up and goes to the kitchen, returning with a patterned box of tissues. I wipe ineffectually at my face with a handful of tissues and then take a long, hiccupy breath.

Teresa perches on the arm of the wingback chair. She pushes my hair out of my face. "Listen to me, Jameson Harper. You are sixteen years old. It's not up to you to solve everyone's problems. It's kind of you, but it's not your job. I think it's way too much pressure to put on a teenager."

"So you think I should cancel on the TV movie thing so Val doesn't freak out?" My voice sounds flat and lifeless.

"Absolutely not. Selfishly, I'd love to invite you to live here. It would be great, and like you say, if Cole leaves, I will really miss him. But I can't do that to your mother, not without a discussion first. So here's what I think we should do. You set up a meeting with your mom, in a neutral location, and I'll be there to advocate for you. Bring Sam, too, if you think it will help to have two of us. We'll back you up and see if we can negotiate a ceasefire. You shouldn't have to handle all of this on your own. I'm so glad you came to me for help."

"Moving in here would be easier," I say, sounding like I did when I was five.

"The best things in life are never easy. We should try this route first. Then we'll talk about other options if Val still refuses to let you do the acting job." She smiles at me. "Okay?"

I think about it for a moment, then nod.

"I have chocolate chip cookie dough ice cream," Teresa says. "And *The Great British Baking Show*. Both are ideal cures for sick days."

Saturday, May 25th

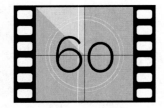

We are sitting in a park halfway between my house and Cole's. A bunch of little kids are playing on the playground nearby, and a handful of dogs run and bark, but we are set back from the noise at a picnic table. I'm on the same side as Val, who sits up straight as if she has a metal rod next to her spine. Sam and Teresa sit across from us. Teresa has brought a brown wicker picnic basket like this might be a happy social occasion.

So far, Teresa and Sam have done most of the talking. My stomach has been tied up in knots the whole time, but they've basically made a case for why I should be allowed to continue working as an actor (I've proven myself to be responsible, I have straight As, I'm trying to save for college and full union status will help with that, my stress level has been dangerously high trying to make everybody happy, etc.). I get the sense that Val is less concerned with my mental health and more concerned with being called out by strangers for her mothering flaws, but they certainly seem to have her attention.

Val is definitely surprised when Teresa tells her she chaperoned me on set when I worked background. She doesn't seem to like this, even though she refused to drive me or stay with me, so that makes no sense in my mind. I notice that she's been swallowing hard a few times and sneaking side glances at me, as if I've gone behind her back. I want to say, "It's not like you gave me a choice," but I'm trying to stay quiet until I'm called on. Sam has been so supportive and sweet, smiling at me from time to time when Teresa is talking. It has taken Val a while to understand the role of a principal talent agent, but Sam is so charming, I think she's slowly winning Val over.

"I appreciate that you both seem to have Jameson's best interests at heart," Val says in response. "I hope that everyone here understands that I want the best for her as well." She pauses while we all murmur and nod. My stomach clenches. "This has been a difficult year so far for me as well. I assume Jameson told you that her father has moved out temporarily and my father, Jamesy's grandfather Butch, has been in the hospital and now has cancer." Her voice wavers, and she takes a moment to gather her thoughts before continuing. I can hear a bird chattering away in a tree above our heads. "I'm feeling overwhelmed right now. I can see that I'm not functioning at my best, and I'd like for Jamesy and me to be closer again." I wonder if I look as shocked as I feel. Val is overwhelmed? Not at her best? And admitting to these things?

Val turns her body toward me. She's still ramrod straight, but her mouth softens, making her eyes appear warmer. "I know I've been hard on you. I do see that. I've been worried about your future, but other than your science mark, I have to admit that you are doing well in school. I keep hoping that acting is only a phase for you, but nearly getting into the performer's union makes it seem much more permanent."

Now I feel ready to respond. Having Sam and Teresa there has propped up my courage, so I decide to tell her how I really feel. "I tried to quit acting. I thought it would make things better between us, and help you and Edward not to fight so much. But it didn't really change anything, except make me unhappy. And I don't want to be unhappy and worried anymore." I glance across the table and see both Sam and Teresa smiling at me, so I continue. "I need to film this TV movie role on Wednesday and Thursday. And go on any auditions that Sam sets up for me. I've come too far and I can't quit now." I pause, and then decide to just say it all. "Oh, and I also want to audition for my school musical. It's not a phase. I'm an actor and this is what I want to do with my life."

I pause, waiting for her to respond. She's looking somewhere beyond me, into the trees. After what feels like a really long time, Val sighs and says, "I see."

(Not exactly supportive or helpful.) I take another deep breath and work at calming down. "I do understand that this has been a shitty time for all of us. I'm terrified every day about Butch, and also about Edward. I'd like to talk about it with you, even the scary things. I'm not Tim. I think we could help each other if you'll talk to me." Val looks at me, thinking over what I've said, but she doesn't say anything. After a minute it gets uncomfortable, and I can feel myself getting hot around my neck.

"Something has to change between us, Mom. I'll move out if we are going to keep fighting about this. Or Cole. I don't want to fight about him anymore, either. I love him and he's fantastic and I don't want to hide my boyfriend from you. I have a plan in place, and I'm ready to move out if things aren't going to change." My breath is coming fast after this bout of honesty, but I suddenly feel lighter, like I might float up into the sky. Holding this shit in has been choking me. I feel my face relax. Teresa squeezes my knee under the table. No matter what Val says, suddenly I think I'm going to be okay.

Val's voice is stretched tight. "You are not moving out of our house. That's ridiculous. We can sort everything out. I'm sure of it."

"I can work on the MOW next week with no grief?" I confirm. "And go on auditions? And date Cole without getting hassled?"

Val takes a long sip from her travel coffee mug. I can see her mind working through this. Maybe we are more similar than I want to think we are, because if the tables were turned, I'd be struggling with this public confrontation too. But I can't keep going like this. I have to know that we are going to stop fighting.

Finally, Val looks at me and says, "Yes, Jameson, I think we can work all of this out between us. Let's try to be more honest with each other. It's been a rough patch, but we can get through this."

I give her a small smile but don't know exactly what to say in response. Edward always says that in sales, you stop talking when you get the answer you want. I'd rather have a big, warm, comforting hug like I got last night at Teresa's, but I know it's not Val's style. We have a long way to go, but at least I can work next week and stop agonizing over letting Sam down. I never would've been able to do this without Sam and Teresa's help.

Teresa pulls the picnic basket closer and starts taking out a glass thermos of lemonade, some decorative cups, and a container of brownies. Sam hands me the script for the TV movie and we all start eating.

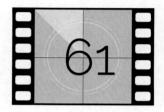

EXT. FARMER'S MARKET — DAY

JAMESON HARPER as MOLLY (16) walks with TOM (18) through stalls of flowers and organic jam.

> TOM
> You are going to win for the best strawberry jam. I just know it.

> MOLLY
> (bright smile)
> I learned from the very best.

Tom and Molly stop at a stall where Molly's mom, GENEVIEVE (38) stands in an apron that reads "Mollyberry Jam."

> GENEVIEVE
> You two better hurry, the judging should be starting soon.

> MOLLY
> We want you to come with us. If I win, it's because of you.

Genevieve smiles at Molly, then removes her apron and lays it on the table next to the jam. She walks around the booth and the three of them walk away, all holding hands.

                    DIRECTOR (O.S.)
          Cut! Moving on.

                    →←

Edward and I are at crafty while the crew sets up the next shot. I feel a surge of happiness, like I'm plugged into adrenaline, and I can't believe how close I was to missing out on this. Sure, the dialogue might be a touch cornball, but I'm here on set, doing what I've dreamed of doing for the last few years. It feels so right, and I'm enjoying that for as long as it lasts.

"Mac and cheese! With breadcrumbs on top!" Ed's like a kid at the carnival every time we wander over to crafty. Teresa came with me as my chaperone yesterday, and today Ed has taken the day off work to stay with me. As we are loading up our plates, my phone buzzes. It's a text from Cole.

> Thinking about you today. Is it fun? Call me anytime. I miss you and want to see you

I don't know how to respond. It's too hard to think about him leaving, plus he's swamped with school right now, so I'm keeping my contact with Cole short and to the point.

> It's SO fun. Miss you too

As a message, it looks sad and bears no resemblance to our flirty communication before he started talking about moving to Calgary. I keep thinking about how Teresa told me that I can't fix everything. Some things are beyond me. I'm determined not to take on everyone's work for them. If Cole wants to go, I'm allowed to feel however I feel about it—at least that's what Teresa told me yesterday in my trailer. It sounded good when she said it, but it's very hard in practice. But I can try.

I put my phone away while Ed and I walk to our little black

tent near the farmer's market set. It's hot out, so we pull our director's chairs (real director's chairs!!!) outside the tent and sit in the shade to eat our snack. I've decided to just enjoy the fact that it's slightly easier with Ed right now. Between our pub dinner when I asked for his help and my Val-tervention with Sam and Teresa, he seems looser and more fun (basically, like he used to be when I was younger). I'm trying not to read too much into this, either. I'm going to ride it like a wave while it's here.

I've been texting Lawrence all day, little cheery things to keep him from the dark side. I invited him to come visit me on set, but he said he wasn't up to it. He finally agreed to let me tell Darren what happened with his parents, so Darren has been on Larry-watch along with me. I told Ed today as well, and he surprised me with his level of support. He said he'd never consider kicking me out of the house, over anything.

"This is delicious," Ed says with his mouth full of macaroni and cheese. "I'm having a lot of fun hanging out with you today."

I glance over and smile. "I feel the same. I'm so glad you came."

"The mac and cheese was the big draw."

The second A.D. walks over, gesturing to me. "Jamesy, we need you on set to block the next scene."

I hand Edward my plate, stand up and fix my sky-blue dress, then follow her back to set.

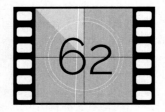

"You sure you are good there, Butch? I can get you some more pillows for that bum leg." We're at Teresa and Cole's because my episode of *Code Breakers* is on network TV tonight. We've all been talking and laughing through it, waiting for me to appear.

Butch waves his hand at Cole. "I'm incredibly comfortable. Don't worry about me." After a few rounds of radiation directed at the tumour by Butch's knee, his leg looks red and sore. Cole and Teresa put Butch in the leather recliner, and we've all been waiting on him hand and foot. He says he wouldn't miss my TV debut party for anything.

Tim is nestled into the same chair with Butch. I like to think he's doing better now with Ed and Val's relationship roller coaster, but a couple of times a week I wake up in the morning with Tim wedged in bed beside me, so obviously he's still worried. Tonight, Ed and Val are out for dinner together to "talk things through," so I'm trying not to read too much into it, but it does seem hopeful. Ed was worried about missing my *Code Breakers* episode, but we've set it up to PVR at home, and I reassured him that this is the first of many (oh please oh please may that be true).

Grace sits on a chair pulled in from the kitchen. She looks fabulous in her glittery skinny jeans and a Grateful Dead concert T-shirt. Grace brought her knitting and has been gabbing with Teresa the whole night.

"Why are you not selling these ginger snaps by the thousands?" Lawrence asks Teresa, who is plying us with enough snacks to feed a hundred instead of the nine who are here. It's been a few weeks since Frank tossed Lawrence out into the street. They haven't spoken, but his mom has texted him once or twice to do a pulse check. His aunt and uncle have been reasonably kind to him, so the shock seems to be wearing off slowly. But I can still see a haunted expression in him that was never there before. Darren is here tonight, and they are cute as can be, cuddling together on one end of the couch.

Brooklyn is the last guest at Cole's viewing party. I wasn't sure if I should invite her, but she told me she "can't wait to celebrate" with me, so I thought I should give her the benefit of the doubt. She's squashed into a beanbag chair next to Butch, and it's amusing watching them catch up and joke around. It feels like old times.

"Are you getting excited?" Cole whispers in my ear. "I can't wait to see you onscreen." He's holding my hand and every nerve in my body is alert and electric. We've been spending so much time together these last couple of weeks, as Cole's senior classes wind down. He's hurtling toward graduation, and quietly making plans with his dad for Calgary, but I've decided to go all-in while I still can. Holding part of myself back wasn't working anyway. I love him and I want him forever, but if I can't have forever, I may as well have as much of him as I can right now.

"I think I should've been in it by now," I confess to Cole at a low volume. We are fifty-four minutes into *Code Breakers* and my character Beekdal has yet to appear. I battle a rising panic that I've been cut completely—all those jaunty, entertaining lines, not to mention my spectacular murder. It was so fun to fake bleed out on the floor by the safe, but maybe somewhere a decision has been made that my little storyline wasn't essential to the plot of this weird new TV show.

"Any minute now, movie star," Butch says with a smile.

"I don't know, everybody," I announce to the room. "I shot four separate scenes, with a murder in the last one, and I'm starting to realize they may have cut out my whole storyline. And you all came to support me, which means so much. This is really embarrassing." My voice begins to waver.

Cole squeezes my hand, then stands up to rescue me. "Well, if they cut your part, that was the stupidest decision ever made in Hollywood."

"Damn straight," calls Butch at the same time as Lawrence shouts, "No shit, man!"

"I've heard of this happening and it's so unfair," Brooklyn chimes in. "You deserve better, Jamesy."

"Maybe it will be on next week instead? We can have a standing *Code Breakers* party here until we see you." I smile at Teresa, even though I feel like a moron.

The room goes quiet for the last few minutes of the episode. We all seem to be hoping I'll suddenly appear, but when the credits roll, it's clear that my big debut has been a total bust. Everyone is ridiculously kind, saying things like, "It's all part of being an actor," and "This happens to everyone," but I feel gutted. Tim makes me laugh, though, when he says, "I knew they'd never put you on TV."

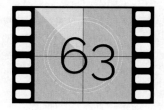

"Do you need any more water here?" the server asks.

I shake my head. "No, I think we're okay." I'm the only one left at our table. The rest of Cole's friends are either on the dance floor or mingling somewhere else (or outside smoking joints or drinking, far away from the teachers who are supposed to be chaperoning). I watch Cole, taking photos with a large group in one of those photo booths with props like fake mustaches and grad signs.

It's strange to be at a grad banquet without graduating. It's like a preview for my own event in two years. Will Cole and I even be together then? Was it worth it to fall in love when we only had these last few months to be together before he takes off? I try not to think about that. There's no point.

To distract myself, I pull out my phone and reverse the camera to check my face. Brooklyn came over this afternoon and did my makeup for me. I paid to have my hair done in an updo. It's curled with a few loose pieces falling near my face. I told Sam I was going back to the same thrift store where we got my peacock dress for Cole's commencement and Sam told me she had been a bridesmaid last year and she had a gorgeous dress I could borrow. I took the bus into the city to try it on. It's cocktail length, a deep burgundy colour with small white swirls in it. I love how the fabric shimmers when I move. When Cole came to pick me up, he told me I looked like a dream come to life. We kissed so much in his car that I worried I'd ruined my makeup, but it was totally worth it. (Thank you, Sam.)

I watch him walk toward me, so handsome in his navy suit. "Hi," he says when he is standing next to me. "Will you dance with me?"

"Love to." He takes my hand, and we weave through the tables at the country club to the dance floor. It smells like sweat and aftershave. Cole pulls me in tight, kissing me on the temple. The song fades out and the band hits the first notes of "Lady in Red." This is an old song, one of Lawrence's '80s-fixation favourites. I feel flooded with happiness.

"Remember all those times we worked together at the Lantern before we started dating?" Cole says. "What a goddamn waste. I should've asked you out the first day I met you."

We shuffle our feet, my head on his shoulder. I think about the first time he held my hand. When we had our first kiss, with Butch in the hospital. How he broke his phone and didn't return any of my texts and I felt like an idiot, but then he came to my door to make sure I was okay. I remember standing in my bra and panties in front of him for the first time, how electric it felt to be skin to skin, exploring each other with our mouths and hands. To be safe and loved and cared for. Chosen. That's how I feel with him.

"Cole, I love you. No matter what."

He moves me out from him slightly so he can see me. "Buddy. I love you, too. No matter what."

He leans down to kiss me. I try to shut out the rest of the world and just be here, with him. I want to hold this moment like a picture in my mind.

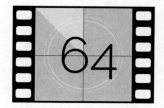

INT. HIGH SCHOOL THEATRE — DAY

JAMESON HARPER as CAPTAIN FUZZY (16), wearing black cat ears, walks in wide circles on the empty stage with a PIANIST (18) accompanying at the piano on stage right.

> CAPTAIN FUZZY
> (singing)
> It's here —this is the moment to decide.
> Do I fight, tallying the cost, or should
> I now surrender…

> MRS. WU (O.S.)
> You must fight, my Captain! Never
> surrender!

> CAPTAIN FUZZY
> (singing)
> But I am old. This may be my last battle.
> Even now, I still feel afraid, not for
> me but for each one of you. My army, my
> soldiers, my family. You are mine, and
> I am yours.

```
                   MRS. WU (O.S.)
   We will fight by your side, Captain
   Fuzzy. And we will triumph!
                   (beat)
   Okay, let's leave it there.
```

The music stops. Jamesy smiles.

```
              MRS. WU (CONT'D; O.S.)
   Thanks, Jamesy. Good job. You can have
   a seat.
```

→ ←

"You did a fabulous job, Jamesy. I'm sure you're going to get Fuzzy." I sit down beside Brooklyn in the theatre, where a group of us are waiting to be called to cold read a scene with Lieutenant Rags (Lawrence is one of the auditioning hopefuls for that role, one I told him he was born to play).

"Thanks. Your audition was great, too, Brooklyn. And I wouldn't count out Rebecca. She's got some dance moves."

Brooklyn whispers, "Yeah, but when she sings it sounds like cats are being tortured. And not in a good way, even for this show." We giggle together, watching as the next Captain Fuzzy hopeful takes the stage.

My phone starts vibrating. Sam is calling. Mrs. Wu has a strict "no cell phones in the theatre" policy, so I tuck it into my pocket and race up the stairs and out of the theatre to answer it.

"Jamesy?" she says in an excited voice.

"Yeah, Sam, I'm here. Thank you so much for your killer dress, by the way. Cole said I looked like a dream and it was absolutely perfect for grad."

"That's fab but not why I'm calling. Are you ready for some amazing news?"

"What?" I say, in spite of my best efforts not to get too excited about acting opportunities. The *Code Breakers* heartbreak is simply too fresh. Does it even count as a credit if I got cut? I applied to the union with my voucher after I worked but I'm too

192 | JULIANNE HARVEY

embarrassed to even ask Sam this question.

"I just got an email from the casting director at *Code Breakers*. She couldn't believe your part got cut and she felt bad for you because she knew it was your first role." Sam's voice is getting faster and faster. "Now here's the amazing bit. She's casting a feature with Amy Poehler and Tina Fey and there's a part as Poehler's daughter that she thinks you'd be suited for. She's setting up an audition for you Friday morning. Can you make it?"

Oh my God. Amy Poehler and Tina Fey are my dream mentors in the acting world—hilarious and smart and brave. I can hear Lawrence in my head, asking why it couldn't be his girlfriend Julia Roberts, but playing Amy Poehler's daughter seems like the ideal role for me.

"Jamesy?" she asks in my ear. "Are you there? Did you hear what I said?"

"Yes, I'm here," I squeak. "I can audition on Friday. I can't think of anything I'd like more."

Thursday, June 27th

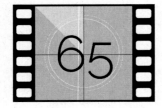

"Happy Birthday to you, happy birthday to you, happy birthday dear Butchie, happy birthday to you!" Butch blows out his candles with dramatic flair (it's clear where I get my acting talent from!) and everyone cheers. I feel a massive lump in my throat when I think about how scary these last few months have been with Butch in and out of hospital with shitty knee cancer, but today he is here, and we are celebrating him.

Val rented out the dining room at Sunny Acres for the festivities, from three to four in the afternoon (when many of the residents are napping). I came early with her and Tim so we could decorate the place. Technically, tomorrow is the last day of school, but I've got my Poehler/Fey audition at eleven a.m. so (miracle of miracles!) Val said I could be finished today. She also said she could drive me for the audition and then I can pick where to go for lunch. I almost fell over dead with shock. I'm sure it's still going to be a long road with her, but she's making an effort and I'm thankful.

So now I'm on summer break. I'm still wearing my shoulders as earrings thinking about Cole driving out to Calgary on Saturday, but he said I have a standing invitation to come visit whenever I want. Who knows—maybe there will be an acting opportunity there. Anything can happen. I'm trying my damn best to remember this as it helps me not fall into despair.

Val cuts slices of lemon cake (my favourite, and Butch's too) and Tim hands them around to all of the guests. Butch sits at his usual dining room table, holding court and entertaining those standing around him. Darren and Lawrence have their arms around each other as they examine the contents of Sunny Acres' locked glass liquor cabinet. Ed is trying to hand Tim napkins to go with the slices of cake but he's taking the plates away too fast which makes Val laugh at Ed's futile efforts. Brooklyn tries to talk to Marty, Tim's new friend from Korea who is here for two years to learn English, and so far only knows words about Xbox that Tim and the rest of his goofy friends have taught him.

"What are you thinking about, buddy?" Cole appears beside me, slipping his tanned arm around my waist.

"I'm thinking that it's close to good right now."

"Maybe that's all we can ever really hope for." He turns me to face him. I'm immediately lost in the green pools of his eyes.

"Close to good is actually pretty great."

Cole's response is to lower his head and kiss me. His mouth is sweet and light on mine. He tastes delicious, like strawberries.

"Gross!" Tim says with two plates of cake thrust out at us. "You're disgusting."

"Yup," Cole agrees. "Thanks for the cake." Tim makes a sour face and runs toward Marty.

We start to eat our cake. It's lemony and tart. Butch gestures for us to come join him. Cole and I both sit down at the table, his bare leg in shorts pressed against mine in a red polka dot mini skirt. Everyone crowds around the table, eating cake, drinking lemonade, and chatting. For this moment, there are no problems that need solving. We are all here. I have no clue what's going to happen next, but that's okay.

It's close to good right now, and that's actually pretty great.

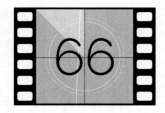

INT. CASTING OFFICE — DAY

JAMESON HARPER (16) walks into the casting office. The CASTING DIRECTOR (35) stands up from behind her table.

> CASTING DIRECTOR
> Jamesy! Thank you for coming in.

> JAMESON
> (grinning)
> Of course. It's my pleasure. I'm thrilled you asked for me.

The C.D. walks to Jamesy.

> CASTING DIRECTOR
> I couldn't believe you got cut from *Code Breakers*. Sam says you took it well, but I'd find that heartbreaking.

JAMESON
(leaning in)
Between you and me, my heart did break.
But it's worth it for the chance to
audition for Tina Fey and Amy Poehler.

CASTING DIRECTOR
That's the right attitude, for sure.
Wild things happen all the time in this
industry.

The C.D. gives Jamesy's arm a light squeeze,
then moves back to her table. She sits down
beside a READER (22), who also operates the
camera.

Jamesy puts down her backpack and shakes out
her hair. She steps on the green tape mark
in front of the camera. Jamesy closes her
eyes and draws a long, deep breath.

CASTING DIRECTOR
Ready whenever you are.

Jamesy's eyes fly open, and she starts to
speak.

ACKNOWLEDGEMENTS

I wrote this book for my daughter Ava, who complained that I wrote a picture book for her brother William when he was five years old, and I hadn't written anything specifically for her. Well, here is that book —long overdue for sure, but no less a labour of love from me to you. Thanks for going after your big dreams with strength and courage, and for all of the many hours we spent together in Vancouver driving around to auditions and doing background work in film and TV. Crafty rocks!

To my editor, Karen Ydenberg White. Not only are you a wizard with words and grammar, you are also a long-time friend. (And you make stellar poolside G&Ts.) Thank you for the cheerleading when I needed it most. Your belief in me made a big difference when my confidence was low. May this only be the first of many book collaborations between us!

Thank you to my talented cover designer and friend Dani Compton. I'll never forget gasping out loud with joy when I saw your design for the Ruby Finch Books logo. I knew then that your keen eye for colour, fonts, and layout meant I had an ideal partner in this publishing venture. I cannot thank you enough for the hours you spent on Jamesy's gorgeous cover. You took my words "simple and stunning" to a whole new level. Working with you is a dream and I'm excited already about the next book cover!

Huge thanks to Patrick O'Connor and the whole First Choice Books team for the design and printing. You were all such a pleasure to work with, from start to finish. I really appreciate your attention to detail and your personal touches. You made this book beautiful.

I'd like to thank Cathleen With, who taught me YA fiction at Kwantlen Polytechnic University. This novel began in her class and she supported it from the very start. So many profs at KPU made a difference in my writing journey, but I specifically want to thank Ross Laird, who taught me Group Counselling at Vancouver Community College more than twenty years ago, and has been such an inspiring and important mentor in my life since then.

I finished my MFA in Creative Writing at UBC just before publishing this novel, so I wanted to shout out to my MFA peeps who kept my head above water in the full-time program (especially Erin, Steve, Edie, Susan, Minelle, Paul, and Stuart). As for faculty, special recognition goes to my kick-ass thesis supervisor Taylor Brown-Evans and my TA supervisor Tanya Kyi —thanks for believing in my abilities when I began to doubt them.

I can't possibly write acknowledgements without thanking Toby Welch, my Alberta Mucho Burrito lunch pal (and writing mentor, editor, cheerleader, and best hugger on planet earth). Thanks for always being there for me. It means a lot.

Big thanks to my husband Jason and my kids Ava and William (plus of course the two best cats around, Teddy and Flower). Thanks for reading for me and supporting me as a writer and now a publisher. I love you all so much. Laughing with you is the absolute best.

To the librarians and teacher-librarians who have supported this novel, I thank you from the bottom of my heart. Libraries are central to democracy, and I will defend them until my final breath. I've been a library patron since I was a young child, and I'm forever grateful for every one of the books, DVDs, puzzles, and materials I've borrowed over the last five decades.

And lastly, I thank you, the reader. Thanks for picking up this book and giving me your time. I hope you keep going after every one of your dreams, even if those you love struggle to understand them. Big dreams are worth the effort and the cost. Keep on dreaming.

13096646R00114